Clod
Makes
A
Friend

David J. Pedersen

Odysia Press

Cover art by:
Alessandro Brunelli

Editing by:
Bryan Thomas Schmidt
Danielle Fine

© 2018 Odysia Press
First Edition

ISBN: 978-0-692-04566-4

Dedication

To my parents

Also by David J. Pedersen

Age 9

"Is his name really Clod?" Learned Yugen asked, speaking each word slowly as though the conversation was already a waste of his time. He finished with a distraught sigh, as haughty as his tone.

Clod cursed under his breath—another thing he would get in trouble for, if they could hear him from the other room. Not that it really mattered. His punishment was already going to be severe; how could a little cursing make it worse? It was just so frustrating. Why would his teacher ask that? Was Yugen trying to make this last longer just to torture him? It grated that his teacher would choose to start his visit by picking on Clod's name. His own name was no better. What was a Yugen, anyway? It sounded like the name of a bad noodle. Even worse, the man insisted that everyone pronounce his title "learn-ed," even though it was spelled "learned." As if the extra syllable made him that much more important.

Despite everything Clod had learned in his short nine years, nobody would explain why Yugen's title required the separate '-ed.' The second time Clod had asked, he'd received a sharp rap on the knuckles by Learn-ed Yugen's "teaching wand." The wand had never actually produced any magic he was aware of, other than entrancing the wary eyes of students cautious of its smacking. Clod hated that wand almost as much as he hated his stodgy teacher. He could only imagine that the evil wand was dancing before his mother's eyes right now while Yugen explained the "situation."

Maybe she would break it. His mum had a temper, and Clod listened closely, longing with every fiber of his body to hear the snap of that wand. He kneaded a small mass of clay as he let the scenario play out in his mind. Yugen would gasp, completely speechless as he gawked at the destruction of his favorite disciplining weapon. The pompous man would stomp around in a fit then Clod would rush into the room and hug his mum before they shooed Learn-ed Noodle away. That would certainly make everything better.

"He's named after his father," she said, with absolutely no apology in her voice. It wasn't quite the delicious snap he'd hoped for, but he was grateful for her defiance.

"Eidy, his father's name was Claude, with a *u* and an *e*. Not an *o*," Learned Yugen corrected, education dripping from his tongue. "So, I'm to assume you can't read or write. This, at least, explains the boy's ignorance."

"What difference does it make?" his mum asked.

"Your illiteracy has cost your son his dignity. Now and forever, he will be known as Clod," Learned Yugen said. "Which is nothing more than a clump of dirt."

Her slight intake of breath was enough for Clod to smash the clay pile with his large fist. It seeped into the pores of the wooden board it sat on. The kids at school had teased him about his name for years, calling him mudboy or dirt-eater. Until now, he'd kept the misspelling from his mother, because she would be hurt too. All she did was work and take care of him. The last thing he wanted was to make her feel bad. Clod thought that punching Learned Yugen in the mouth might make him feel better. He was almost as big as his thin, gaunt teacher, and it wouldn't take much to hurt him. Not to mention, he deserved it. The man was a bully, just like the kids at school, but his mum said no fighting. Even when someone deserved it.

"I am beginning to understand your son's disinterest in the importance of our institution," Yugen went on. "Despite my efforts, he is almost failing in every course."

His grades? Clod's heart raced. Yugen wasn't here to talk about the accident? He had mentioned the accident at school to his mum, hadn't he? It didn't matter; Clod had definitely forgotten to mention his grades. Sort of forgotten. It wasn't that he didn't try to do well; he just didn't get it. Learned Yugen spoke down to him, and he couldn't ask his mum for help. She couldn't read, and she worked so hard at the mill that he just didn't want to bother her with it.

"So, he's passing?" she asked.

Clod immediately wanted to hug her. His mum may be upset with him later, but she was standing up for him now. The evilest teacher ever didn't stand a chance!

"He is," Yugen said. "Barely."

"I live on barely," she said snappily.

"I've noticed," he scoffed.

"It doesn't matter as long as he passes, right?" she said, ignoring the man's slight. "He could still be...chosen?"

"Is the boy here now?" Yugen asked.

"He's resting in the other room. I believe he's sleeping," she said softly. "He was very upset when he came home."

"There's another room? I thought that was a closet," the hateful man muttered, his whiny voice crawling under the door like a freshly hatched nest of spiders. "It is unlikely that Clod could be placed into a school of magic. Amongst his age group, I have already identified those with great talent in Neuromancy, Theriomancy, Chaomancy, Theomancy..." Learned Yugen wasted a lot of air listing a boring variety of '-mancys' other students could perform.

Clod lay on his side, squeezing the pile of clay

that was far more important than anything his teacher had ever said. Despite her long hours at the mill, his mother always managed to bring him an apron-full of clay every few weeks. She would deliver it with an apology about not giving him better toys. But, he really didn't care. Clod loved the clay; it could become anything. He'd made castles they could live in, tiny armies that would protect them, and monsters that could easily be squished. Clay wasn't just a toy; it was all of the toys!

"...and unfortunately, Clod shows less sign of having magic than he does intelligence," Yugen said, interrupting him from clay daydreams. "I doubt you remember from your own school days, but everyone on Yulth can do some sort of magic. The type of magic is typically passed down from the parents. What is your talent?"

"I have none," she muttered.

Clod had never thought of that before, but his mum had never done anything magical, other than make him feel better after a bad day. That certainly had to be a type of "mancy". It should be called "Mum-mancy". She had to be the best mumancer who'd ever existed.

"Pfft," Yugen said. "Everyone has a magical talent. Apparently, you are lacking the same confidence and conviction as your son. Any gift you had is probably so far buried by now that *I* can't even sense it."

"You can't sense any magic in Clod?" she asked, sounding worried.

"None, which is my concern," Yugen said. "I know what each of my students can do the minute they enter my classroom. My efforts are mostly spent teaching those with great potential how to become strong in their magic. I prepare them for a higher education in one of the great cities where they will learn mastery over their power. I also watch for those who are in danger of being tainted by the dark."

"What?" she snapped.

"It's probably nothing to be concerned about. Your son can't even cast the most remedial spells. Usually the weak ones are most tempted by the darkness because it can give them some of that power they lack, but like a disease it will twist a mind to evil." Yugen sighed. "I'm not too concerned. So far, he has done nothing more than live up to his name."

"Oh," his mum said, a hint of defeat in her tone.

"It's not just that," Yugen said, now sounding elated. "He has no friends. The other children are frightened of him. Not only because he is so large, but because he is ugly. They look on him like he's a monster."

"He...he doesn't have a single friend?" she asked.

"No," Learned Yugen said with the empathy of a coroner.

There was despair in her shaky voice, and it was crushing. Clod tried masking a sob by sniffing deeply. The sound of his mum's shame burned into his chest as he clawed at clay bits now smashed into the wooden board. He'd tried so hard to make friends, to play their games, to be nice. It just never went right. Still, more than anything, he wanted a friend. Grasping the mass of clay, he squeezed with all his strength. The clay was firm enough to resist his anger. He opened the palm of his hand and stared at the gray bit of earth.

"Is this why you're here?" his mum asked, the sadness in her voice turned sour. "To insult our house? To insult my son? It sounds like you've already decided he isn't fit for placement in any school of magic. Why should he even bother with your dumb school?"

"I'm here because of what happened on the schoolyard," Yugen explained. "But I think it's just as important you understand what I do. I ed-u-cate. I teach those little vessels of power how to use their gifts wisely, and steer them away from the taint of darkness. Despite my low expectations, your son still could have some small morsel of potential. Something even I don't recognize. It's my job to find that gift and cultivate it. There are not many Learn-ed because it is so rare to recognize and hold an understanding for all forms of magical divination. It is my job to teach those who will become heroes and leaders, weed out the dangerous, and find chores for the few who are less fortunate."

"Less fortunate?" she asked.

"Those, like yourself, and probably Clod, who

lack the conviction to meet their potential," he said with mock regret. "People who will help with the menial tasks of mill work or digging ditches."

There was a long pause, and Clod could practically sense her glaring at Yugen through the closed door.

"Is that all?" she asked coldly.

"That is not all," Learned Yugen continued. "Your oaf of a son is also a menace. Today, he broke young Ried's arm."

"Clod mentioned something about an accident," his mum said. "That someone tripped him, and he fell on Ried."

"And we're all grateful that Ried wasn't crushed," he said. "That boy is a fount of potential. It would have been a great loss."

"My son didn't mention the broken arm. I'm sorry Ried was hurt," she said. "Boys and girls get hurt playing. That's what healers are for. Is Ried in trouble for teasing my son?"

"I don't punish strength," Yugen said sharply.

"Well, you certainly don't inspire confidence," his mum said, her voice louder with every word. "Didn't you just tell me that's what Clod needs?"

The argument that commenced became less important than the clay. Clod smiled as that familiar earthy smell, like a spring rain on dry dirt, filled the room. He worked the mass until it was warm, almost unnaturally so. Something felt different this time—different from all the other times. Normally, he would mold the clay into soldiers, and daydream them to chase Yugen away. This time, the clay seemed to want a shape of its own. Despite his clay-smashing-tantrum, there was still enough to form a pillar. That was when he started to sculpt.

When his thick fingers became too tacky, Clod poked and carved the figure with small sticks he'd fashioned into tools. He frowned in concentration, sweat dripping from his nose at the effort. Frustration became tactile and poured into the tiny figure as his creation evolved into something more. It was the hardest thing he'd ever done, and the most rewarding.

The front door banged hard enough to shake the small cottage. His mum roared in anger, her shoes clacking loudly on the wooden floor as she stormed around. She muttered curses he'd never heard before, and slammed a pot on the stove. Her sobbing made him wince, and he knew he should go apologize, but he wasn't done.

"Dinner," she called after a long while.

He barely heard her, so close to being finished that nothing else mattered. An odd sense of giddiness overwhelmed him, like he was finally doing something right. Like he was discovering something new. His heart fluttered with a hint of confidence that he barely recognized.

The bedroom door opened with a wrenching sound as old wood complained loudly, scraping across the floor with every jolt of his mother's shoulder. He didn't look up when she came in, but felt her eyes watching him work the clay.

"Do you want to tell me more about what happened?" she asked gently.

Her pity struck him. Clod wanted to cry alone more than he wanted to talk about it. After a long wait, he realized she wasn't going away. She sat on the nearby bed, her thin arms crossed but her face and eyes patient. His mum's dark red hair curled about her shoulders. She was thin from too much work and not enough food, but showed no age in her porcelain features. Despite her petite frame, she was strong enough to hold up the world, and far smarter than Learn-ed Yugen gave her credit for. She also had a temper that Clod would have to face if he didn't explain.

"I didn't mean to break his arm," he said through a scratchy throat. "We were playing tag. I think someone tripped me."

"Oh," she said, more concerned than angry. "He's much smaller than you..."

"Everyone is," he said, unable to hold back a tear. It dripped from his chin and landed in the clay. "That's why they make fun of me. They say mean things about my size, and my name, and my face. They tease me all the time for having no magic. Now they'll hate me even more."

"We've talked about being careful playing with the other children," she said gently. "It's hard, but you have to ignore them."

"I just wanted some friends, but they call me names, and push me, and trip me," he said through labored breaths. "It really was an accident, Mum."

10

"I know, baby," she said.

He crawled around his small creation and fell against his mother's legs. She patted his wiry, brown hair as he wept, letting him mumble on about mean kids and wanting a friend of his own. She rocked as best she could until his cries became the occasional catch, finally wiping away his tears with a kerchief before dabbing her own eyes.

"Show me what you're making today," she said, her voice more cheerful. "Is it a dragon, or an army?"

"No, I made a friend," Clod said with a sniff. He turned the board around so his mum could have a better view.

"Oooh," she said, leaning in to look closer. "This is wonderful. You've never made anything so detailed."

The clay figure was shaped, more or less, like a young girl. It stood no taller than his hand, with dark holes for eyes, and a mouth that looked like a shadowy cave. The figure had roughly hewn hair that fell below her shoulders, a round nose, and a dress that draped over her knees.

"What's her name?" she asked.

"My name is Ada," the clay girl squeaked in a tiny voice. Her dark eyes blinked as if she were waking abruptly, and she smiled at Clod.

"Oh my," his mum said with a start, placing a hand on her chest.

It felt right, and Clod beamed at his mum.

She looked from him to the clay figure nervously. "Ada is a very pretty name," his mother said. "Where did you come from?"

Ada raised an arm and aimed it at Clod, her hand so roughly carved she was unable to point. He nodded proudly, slightly out of breath. He'd rarely seen his mum surprised, or even nervous, but her eyes were wide and her hand shook. Despite his elation, he began to worry that he'd done something wrong.

"I see," she said. "And why are you here?"

"To be Clod's friend," Ada said.

And, for some reason, this made his mother's shoulders lower. Her breath caught, but she gathered her composure quickly.

"Well, I'm glad you're here," she said to Ada. "Clod needs a good friend."

"I'll be his best friend," she said sincerely.

"How did I do this, Mum?" Clod asked, staring at Ada in wonder as she spun about. "Yugen said I have no magic."

"Yugen doesn't know everything. But this needs to be our secret," his mother said in her almost-angry voice. "Please, Clod. You can't tell anyone."

"I promise, Mum," Clod said, not completely understanding.

"I'm going away already," Ada said weakly, covering her face with a tiny arm. "But I don't want to go. I need to play with Clod. This isn't enough time."

Ada struggled to say something, but her body became still.

"Ada?" Clod asked.

She didn't move, and he gently rested a finger on her. His heart pounded, and he wanted to cry again. His only friend was already gone. Clod looked at his mother, but she merely shook her head. He wanted to bring her back, but didn't know how. He pulled back his hand, and Ada collapsed into a heap of soft, gray ash.

Age 11

"Mum? Mum. Mum! Mum. Mum! *Mum*!"

"What?" she muttered, her eyes opening as reluctantly as the bedroom door.

"Are you awake?" Clod asked.

"No," she said, rolling away, deeper into her blanket cocoon.

"Mu-umm," he whined, tugging at the blankets.

"Breakfast later," she said.

"Tell me more about my dad," he pleaded. "Did you say he was a sculptor?"

The mass of blankets rose slightly with her intake of breath. She yawned, stretching like a cat, and sighed deeply. "I'm sorry, Clod," she said, rolling back over to face him. Her fine, red hair was a mess of knots and her eyes were red and blotchy. "I probably said too much last night."

"That's because you were drinking," he said, excited to surprise her with that bit of knowledge.

"You always talk a lot when you drink."

"I probably did too much of that, too," she said. "Didn't I tell you everything?"

"I don't know," he asked. "Did you?"

"No," she said softly. "But the rest can wait until later. Much later."

"Not later," he said in frustration. "Now!"

"What would you like to know?" she asked with a patient smile.

"Stop it. Quit tugging at my leg," he said, looking down at his feet. Clod faced his mum. "Did he really make stuff, like me?"

"As I told you, your father was a sculptor," she said, placing a warm hand on his cheek. "Like you, he made stuff."

"Could he have made Ada?" Clod asked in excitement.

"Yes," a squeaky voice cried up from his feet. "Could he have made me?"

Ada was too small to reach the bed. He bent over and gently lifted her to the edge of the thin mattress. She was solid, like one would expect from a mass of clay, but lighter, and warm with life.

"Be careful, Clod," she warned. "You'll squish me again."

"Don't say clod like you're talking about dirt," he snapped defensively.

The clay girl rested a tiny hand on his finger, her face worried. "I didn't mean it like that, I promise."

"Okay," he said, his hurt washed away by her

15

touch.

He was very proud of Ada, more than ever. She was taller than last time, reaching almost a foot, with much greater detail. As she had requested, on many occasions, her dress now fell to her ankles. Ada had more definition in her hands and feet, though many of her features were still too angular to appear natural. It still frustrated him that no matter what he did, her eyes and mouth were dark holes. She still looked like clay, and smelled like clay, but he had done one thing that had earned him a hug. Ada's hair was now brown.

It had taken two years to figure out how to imbue the clay with even the smallest amount of color. Dyes had been a disaster, both to Ada and his mother's kitchen. He'd tried painting her, but ended up getting more paint on himself than her sculpture—and when she woke, it all disappeared. His mum had suggested focusing on just one thing rather than trying to change all of Ada. Ada had requested her hair.

It had been a good week. School was on break, which meant no mean kids, and his anticipation of seeing Ada had boosted his morale. He could practically hear her say, "You can do it, Clod!" So he wished and willed, until finally, the gray was replaced with a rich brown. It was much curlier than his mother's, and not quite the same color, but he'd made it look almost real.

"Oh my," his mother said, gently stroking Ada's hair with a finger. "I see you've been busy,

Clod."

Clod said nothing, but was elated that she'd noticed. Ada arched her back and smiled.

"You look lovely, Ada," Eidy said.

"Thank you, Miss," Ada said, holding out the sides of her dress with a slight curtsy.

"To answer your question, no," his mother said. "I don't believe anyone but you could make Ada."

He smiled so much it hurt. Ada patted his hand excitedly.

"Would he..." Clod began. "Would he be proud?"

"Very," his mum said mid-yawn.

"Did he ever make anyone live?" he asked. "Like I can?"

"What time is it?" she asked, her voice thick with morning.

"I dunno," Clod said. "The sun's been out for a little while."

She looked at Ada thoughtfully and shook her head. When her eyes met Clod's, her mouth curled up in the tiniest of smiles. "Would you like to go outside and play with your friend?" she asked.

Every question about his dad was forgotten. Ada's head whipped around to look at Clod. Her tiny eye-holes widened, and she nodded in excitement.

"But...but, I thought you said we weren't supposed to go outside and play?" he asked, nervous of some unknown danger his mother had forgotten to share.

Ada elbowed his hand and glared as if he'd already spoiled everything. For two years, they'd been told to stay at home, and there had to be a reason. What if rock goblins or tree pixies were known to steal away clay girls and eat them? Not to mention, this was such a surprise, he needed to know if it was true.

"You can now, this once," his mum said. "But please, stay close. And don't let anyone see Ada."

Ada yelped as he grasped her in a hand and ran out the door before his mum could change her mind. There was a pinch in his finger as the clay girl bit down. He loosened his hold with a grunt.

"That hurt," he said, pushing through the wooden door of their home.

"Sorry, but I couldn't see," she said. "I've never been outside, and…and…oh."

A thin, dry snow covered the ground like a sheet of ice, crunching noisily beneath every footstep. The surrounding forest felt close; branches that were normally out of reach hung low from the weight of snow and ice. A carpet of white covered the path leading from their house, making it almost impossible to see. The gentle creak of tree limbs was the only sound that broke the eerie silence of their woodland surroundings.

Clod took in a deep breath of air that smelled crisp and fresh, then let it out in a huff of steamy breath. Ada's eyes widened in amazement, and she breathed out as much as she could, grabbing at the cloud while it passed through her fingers.

"Please," she said. "Set me down."

He scanned the nearby woods for any sign of danger before gently placing her on a patch of snow. She looked down, lifting one foot then the other in a sort of slow march.

"What is that? Are my feet cold?" she asked with wide, excited eyes.

"You…you can feel?" he asked. "Are you okay? I think I can make you shoes."

"I feel the cold, but just a little," she said, wiggling her toes. "It doesn't hurt, at least not right now. Maybe I need shoes next time!"

"Okay," he said, feeling a little giddy.

Like a field mouse, Ada ran a short distance, jumped over a stick, and landed in a small pile of leaves and snow. She rolled over and over, giggling in delight as snow and dirt were thrown about in her fearsome attack. Completely covered beneath the debris, she stopped moving, and his heart skipped. She was so still that he worried their time together was over already. She normally lasted part of a day, sometimes even into the evening. It was unusual for her to go away so soon, and his happiness was starting to leak out like water from a rusty bucket. Especially since this was their first time outside together.

"Ada?" he asked, shuffling forward, careful not to step on the clay girl.

He moved in inches, painfully aware of his enormous feet, until finally reaching the pile of snow and leaves that had swallowed her. He leaned over close to the ground, gingerly poking a

19

finger into the mass and stirring it like a spoon in soup.

"Please don't go yet," he said softly.

"Boo!" The clay girl popped out of the snow and kissed him on the nose.

He gasped, reeling back in shock. A wary smile snuck across his face, happy that they could continue their adventure, but he was also frustrated that Ada had teased him like that. She laughed and laughed while he stood there in his own discomfort.

"That wasn't funny," he said, hurt that she would tease him so. "Now you're picking on me like the other kids."

"No, Clod," she said. "Not like the other kids. They say mean things and push you around. I surprised you, that's all. Friends tease in good ways."

"I guess," Clod said. He was slow to recover, but always appreciated it when she referred to him as a friend.

"You must have other friends who tease you in good ways," she said. "When do I get to meet them?"

"I, uh, I…" He didn't know what to say, and couldn't come up with anything better than the truth. "I don't have any other friends."

"What?" she asked, almost accusingly.

"It's true," he said, his cheeks warming. "I don't. You're my only friend."

"But I only get to see you every three weeks or so," she said. "What do you do when I'm not there?"

"I wait," he said. "I practice making you more…better."

"You're amazing," she said, spinning in place. Her dress flowed lithely around her. "And I love my hair. Thank you, Clod. You did wonderfully."

"You're welcome," he said, glancing up from the ground.

"Clod," she said, her smile wavering. "Why don't you have any friends? Other than me?"

His warmth and excitement suddenly cooled. In the privacy of the small cottage, he rarely had to explain himself to Ada. He would spend three weeks sculpting her, pouring his heart into his creation until she finally woke. They would spend their day talking, playing games, and being friends. Now, out here, in the open, he feared she would come to realize why nobody else liked him. He feared she would leave him if she knew the truth.

"I dunno," he said, shuffling his feet.

"Clod," she said, tugging on the hem of his pants. "Tell me."

There was something about having a friend, a real friend, that made it impossible to hold back. It made him feel queasy, like lying to his mother. She deserved to know, even if it hurt, and so he muttered it as quietly as he could.

"I couldn't hear you," Ada said.

"I'm ugly, okay," he snapped, shaking her off his leg.

She flew from his leg and smashed against a

tree, sticking to it. Clod rushed to her.

"I'm sorry," he said, unable to hold back the tears. "I'm so sorry. I'm so big and clumsy, I just hurt everyone. That's why nobody likes me."

She blinked several times before jerking her head away from the tree bark. His fingers were too thick to pry her free without doing more damage to the clay.

"Please don't leave," he said.

"It's okay," she said, her voice shaky. "It's not time yet. Just give me a moment."

With a tiny grunt, she wrenched one arm free as though it were stuck to a cobweb. She pulled the second arm loose before grasping a leg. He watched helplessly as she pried both legs from the tree and dropped to the ground. Ada stood, dusted herself off, and looked up at him.

"Why are you crying?" she asked, the dark circles of her eyes forming a frown. "I said it was okay."

"Because I hurt you," he said with a deep sniffle. "I hurt everyone. It's always an accident. I never mean it. I'm big, and I'm ugly, and I hurt people. And now I hurt you, and you won't want to be my friend."

Clod couldn't hold back the tears. Ada was his only friend, and now she was going to leave him because he was a monster...

"I don't think you're ugly, Clod," she said.

"I need to make your eyes better," he said with a sniff.

She giggled, which was his favorite.

"I'm sorry if I hurt you," he said.

"It only hurt a little," she said. "It was an accident, but you need to be careful."

He nodded, sniffing loudly.

"And you need to stop crying," she said, crossing her arms.

"Wut?" he asked in surprise. "I thought I was going to lose you."

"Well, I don't think I'm going to die," Ada said. "And I'm not going to stop being your friend for doing something dumb."

"That's not nice," he said.

"Neither was kicking me into a tree," she said firmly. "It's okay to feel bad, Clod, but then you get over it."

He brushed snow off a fallen tree and slumped onto it. "The other kids are mean to me all the time. It's hard to get over it."

"It shouldn't be," she said.

"What do you mean?" he asked.

"Do you like them?" she asked.

"No," he said with a frown.

"Do they mean anything to you?" she asked. "If they left, would you miss them?"

"Definitely not," he said.

"Then their words shouldn't mean anything to you either," she said, crossing her arms.

"Yeah," he said, wiping his nose.

"You're not ugly, Clod," she said.

"You just say that because I made you," he said.

"Do you think I'm ugly?" Ada asked.

"No," he said. "You're as beautiful as my mum."

"That's a sweet thing to say," she said with a broad smile. "But why do you say you're ugly?"

"Just look at me," he said, gesturing to himself with both hands. "I'm taller than all of the other kids my age, and fat. My cheeks droop, my hair is scraggy, and my teeth are jagged. One kid said my eyes look dull, like me. I talk slow, so people think I'm stupid. I'm so clumsy, I hurt everyone. I'm a monster."

"Who told you this?" Ada asked, stomping a foot and placing fists on her hips.

"Ried and other kids in my class," he said, his voice trailing off.

"And you believe them?" she asked.

He said nothing, instead pretending his feet were interesting.

Ada fell back into the snow and stared up at the cloudy sky.

"It's a pretty night," Ada said. "The moon looks beautiful."

"What are you talking about?" he asked. "It's morning."

"No, it's night," she said firmly, pointing to the clouds. "Don't you see the stars?"

"No," he said, glancing at the sky. "Maybe you hit your head too hard against the tree."

"So, I'm your friend, and you don't believe me that it's night?" she asked.

"No," he said. "You're not making sense."

"But you believe the bullies at school when

they say you're ugly," she said.

"Well…" his voice trailed off.

She stared at him, for a long while, but said nothing.

"Let's do something fun," she said.

"Yuh," he agreed, grateful for the change in conversation. "We should visit the big cave by the sea. It's at the edge of our property so no one is ever there. Mum says it's filled with trolls, but I think she's just trying to scare me so I don't go."

"We should do that someday," she said. "But I want to visit your town."

"Really?" he asked in surprise. "But mum said no one should see you."

"Then we'll be sneaky," she said. It was hard to make out her expression, but her voice sounded full of mischief. "First, fix my back. I don't think it's right."

She turned around, and he winced. Bark from the tree had left a hollow indentation between her shoulders that would've been grotesque if she were human. He wasn't sure what to do or if he could even fix Ada while she was awake. But he would try.

"Wait here," Clod said, rushing back to the cottage. He returned with a handful of clay, squeezing and warming it with his large hand until it was malleable. "I'm not sure if this will work, so hold still."

"Okay," Ada said, sounding a little worried.

He gently pressed a bit of clay into her back,

and it immediately fell off. The second try didn't stick, nor did the third.

"Ouch," she said. "Not so rough."

"Sorry." He harrumphed. "I don't understand why it's not working."

"I'm not completely clay when I come to visit," she said, trying to look at the damage over her shoulder. "I change when you use your magic."

"Oh," Clod said. He never completely understood how she came to be, he just sort of did it. His magic was mostly depleted by the time she woke up, and he definitely didn't have enough to start from scratch, but maybe there was a little bit left.

"I'll try one more time," he said. "I promise to be gentle."

"Okay," Ada said bravely. Facing forward, she squeezed her eyes shut and balled up her tiny fists. "You can do it."

Clod closed his eyes and tried focusing on those thoughts that brought her to life. It had started with the desperation of loneliness. Then that hunger for a friend would grow into something more. Anticipation of their short time together. Excitement for their adventures. A warmth that filled his heart, like when he thought of his mum. Sweat trickled down his cheeks, and he gasped, opening his eyes. The clay in his hand radiated that same, living warmth Ada did. He knelt and gently pressed it into her back, her arms, and her legs. It was harder to mold her shape without more time or the sticks he used as tools, and his large fingers fumbled awkwardly.

"That tickles," she giggled.

"Oh," he said with a grin. "You're ticklish now?"

She laughed and pulled away as he poked her side once more.

"It's not like it was," he said. "But you're patched up."

"I feel better," Ada said, turning around. "Thank you."

He nodded, rubbing the remaining clay off on his coarse pants. It immediately turned to ash as his magic dissipated, and Clod patted it away.

"Do we still have enough time to see the town?" he asked.

Her face scrunched cutely, and she looked up at the sky in concentration. "I think we have even more time."

"Huh," he said, scratching his cheek.

"Let's goooo!" she said excitedly.

"Follow me," he said.

He led slowly, letting her tiny legs set the pace, and being oh-so-careful with her underfoot. His heart still hurt that he'd damaged her, and he couldn't bear for it to happen again. Ada may have forgiven him for what he'd done, but that didn't mean she liked it.

Fifteen minutes later, they broached the edge of the woods, where the path to his home met a cobblestone sidewalk. Ada gasped, gripping his pants as she reeled at the sight. Clod reveled in being able to introduce his friend to something new.

"Welcome to Durgoon," he said with a bow and a flourish.

"Ooh," she said, gawking all around in wonder.

His heart thrummed in his ears as she looked up and down the street. It was peacefully quiet, being far too early for even the greediest of merchants. What he'd always taken in stride, Ada took in with gasps. The stone road was moist from melted snow, and wide enough to allow the passage of several wheeled carts. Her round eyes and dropped jaw made him look about. Sidewalks of cobblestone framed both sides of the road, and every hundred feet stood a black pole with a lantern that glowed brightly in the early morning haze. Glass-windowed shops along the sidewalks displayed food, and drink, and clothes, and everything Ada had never seen.

"Is the whole world like this?" Ada asked.

"No." He chuckled. "Most of Yulth is woods, and mountains, and oceans. This is just one town in the kingdom of Pag."

"There are more?" she asked in wonder. "Can we see those too?"

"Lots more," he said. "But most are even more boring than Durgoon. It's probably a little more exciting here since it's a port town. We get a lot of ships and traders, but that just means people are busy and rude all the time."

"Oh," she said.

"But maybe someday we should go to a city,"

he said, trying to keep up her excitement. "There are six in Pag, the biggest being the capital. They are huge, with more people than you can count. Mum says that's where all the money from the towns go, so everything is beautiful."

"Maybe we should go there now," she said, practically jumping up and down.

"It takes days to get to a city. We should probably go home," he whispered. "People will be up and about soon."

"No way," she said. "We just got here. Quit being a ninny."

"I'm not a ninny," he said.

"Let's go there," Ada said, pointing at a bakery. She scrambled across the street before he could stop her.

"Wait," he said, a little too loudly. He followed her as she approached the window. "You've got to be more careful."

"No one is here to see us," she said.

"But horses and carriages cross that road all the time," he said in concern. "They'd make a mess of you!"

"What's that?" she asked, pointing at the window.

"Cake," he said longingly. "It's cake."

It wasn't merely cake being displayed in the window, it was art. This confectionery was known to produce the finest, most beautiful, most expensive cakes in all of Durgoon. The cake stood in three tall layers of succulent red frosting thick and solid-looking as any wall. Yellow frosting laced the edges in loops that circled flowers of even more frosting. He'd never taken the time to look, and now couldn't pull his eyes away.

"What is cake?" she asked.

"The best thing ever," he said loftily.

"And…."

"You eat it," Clod, dragging his eyes away to glance at Ada. He suddenly realized that she'd never eaten anything. "You put it in your mouth, and it tastes wonderful. When you eat enough, you feel great. If you eat too much, you feel sick but still want more."

"That sounds amazing," she said.

"It really is." He nodded vigorously.

"I want some," Ada said firmly.

"Me too," he said. "But they aren't open, and I don't have any money…"

"I want some now," she snapped, pushing at the door.

"Yeah, so do I," he said with a grin.

Ada walked to the middle of the door, shoved roughly, and fell forward. The door had a smaller door that swung from a hinge on top. It was too small for a person, but just right for a pet, and perfect for Ada. She looked back, flashed him a mischievous grin, and then she was gone.

"Ada?" he asked, dropping to his knees before the flap. Panic crawled up his spine and filled his mind with all the different ways they could get in trouble. He couldn't yell louder; he might alert someone on the street. He was big enough to push through the door, but that might wake the owner.

AGE 11

Clod stood and pressed his face against the shop window, trying to see what was going on. A shadowy little figure climbed up a chair and hopped over to the display. She leaned forward, breathing in the deliciousness, both increasing his worry and making him jealous. In all his life, he'd only had cake once, and it was like happiness you could eat.

She lifted a hand over the frosting, ready to dig in. He shook his head, knowing that would be the worst thing she could do. This wasn't just cake, it was perfection, and she would...then she did. The tiny hand dug deep into the wondrous morsel of frosting and produced a handful of bready goodness that she shoved into her mouth. Ada's eyes went wide as she fell back behind the cake, out of sight.

Clod tapped on the glass, and then again. The door creaked open, making him jump back and look up and down the street. The door opened more, and tiny Ada was beckoning him in. He shook his head even as she nodded with cheeks full of cake and her face smothered in red frosting. She was gone again, and he had no choice but to follow.

He'd never made so much noise in his entire life. The hinges of the door needed oil, the wood floor needed nails, and he needed to be light as a feather. Wishing and worry didn't help as every footstep into the bakery seemed louder than the last. When he was finally certain that nobody was rushing into the room, he found Ada sitting on the display, stuffing her face.

"What are you doing?" he whispered loudly.

"It's soooo gooood," she said, shoving handfuls of frosting into her mouth. "Hab sum."

"I can't… We shouldn't," he said, his whispering filled with panic. "We could ruin it, and…"

The cake already looked like it had been attacked by a small animal, and there was far too much damage to fix. Neither his magic, nor the best baker in the city could've repaired that piece of art. He took in a deep whiff of baked goods and was immediately overwhelmed with hunger. Reluctantly, against every ounce of better judgment, Clod reached out with a large finger and dipped it deep into the red pastry. Life had never tasted better, and he was dizzy with wonder. The cake was actually more delicious than it looked.

Footsteps upstairs made time stop. The shop owners. He stood there, dumbfounded, with a tasty finger in his mouth, listening to worried voices.

"What's going on down there!" a woman shouted.

"Gotta go," Clod said.

"Bring the cake," Ada urged.

"What?" he asked.

"We already broke it," she said. "They can't use it anymore. It will go to waste."

That made so much sense that Clod grabbed the top two layers and shoved his way out the door. They ran across the street and down the path, leaving angry voices far behind. His eyes darted to Ada, who moved surprisingly fast for being so small.

"This way," he said, taking a deer trail away from the house.

They rushed through the crunchy snow, giggling at the armful of red cake he held like a baby. After several panicked minutes, they stopped to listen. Nothing. Sweet nothing. Clod carefully pressed his back against a large tree and slowly sat down on a pile of dry leaves. He looked at Ada, who squinted as she listened.

"I think we're safe," she whispered.

"Let's eat," he said.

He could only imagine that this is what a feast for kings and queens would taste like. The sliver of cake his mother had brought him from a party was no match for the red pile of deliciousness that the two delinquents demolished. Clod ate until the cake was gone and his belly distended. Ada's small body lay across the girth of his stomach. She was covered in so much frosting it looked like she'd bathed in it.

"So good," she mumbled, lowering her head to his chest. "Best day ever."

"Yuh," he said through a comforting burp.

A beam of warming sunlight reached through the trees, baking Clod and Ada in sleepy content. Here he was, with a stomach full of cake after spending the morning with his best friend. She was right; this had to be the best day ever. It wasn't even cold out. It was actually…sort of…sleepy…

CLOD MAKES A FRIEND

* * * *

"Get off," Clod said to whoever was nudging his leg. "Leave me be."

The nudge became a kick, sharp enough to make him open his eyes. Sleep had made his vision foggy, and he couldn't quite make out the tall figure hovering over him.

"Get up," Learned Yugen snapped, baring his teeth.

"Wut?" Clod asked, blinking rapidly. He rubbed sleep from his eyes even as his teacher grasped his wrist with his talon-like fingers.

Yugen pulled him to standing, and Clod panicked that Ada may fall from his chest, but she was gone. She was really gone. Ash from her remains powdered his tunic, making him sigh. He smiled, in spite of her departure. He'd never been on such a great adventure. Then Clod winced. No adventure had ever made his stomach hurt so much.

"He's here," Yugen shouted. "I have found him!"

"What's going on?" Clod asked, turning away from his teacher.

"Half the town has been looking for the thief who broke into Haim's bakery," Yugen said vehemently. He placed a hand on both Clod's shoulders and jerked him about so they could see eye-to-eye. "Even if you have no magic, we are connected, boy, as I am with anyone who enters my classroom. That's how I know what my students can do, and that's how I sift through the useless and potentially evil children to find the good ones."

Clod covered his mouth with a hand, barely nodding in acknowledgment of Learned Yugen's greatness.

"It was simple to track you down," he said with a sneer. "You think it would be that easy, breaking and entering like a half-wit? Everyone will finally see what you are."

Clod's head reeled, his stomach churned painfully, and he turned away.

Yugen grabbed his chin and drew it forward. "Look at me when I'm talking to you," he said sharply.

"That's him!" Clod recognized the woman's voice from the bakery.

"Oh, Clod," his mother said from nearby.

"What do you have to say for yourself?" Yugen asked.

Clod opened his mouth and threw up all over his teacher. It spewed out in great clumps as mounds of partly-digested too-much-cake coated Yugen's robes. He hurled again and again until it was finally done. The small crowd that gathered was silent, staring at Clod and Yugen in awe.

"Sorry?" Clod asked. It wasn't really an apology.

Age 14

"Thank you, Mister Haim," Clod said as he stepped out of the warm bakery and into cold spring showers. "Thank you for everything."

After three years of not-so-hard labor, he was officially free from his sins. Breaking into the bakery with Ada had been a gloriously bad adventure, and not without cost. Stealing a cake meant for visiting royals was unforgivable. Clod was too big to spank, maybe even too large for a flogging. Learned Yugen had recommended that a public wailing with a reed would leave the right kind of scars Clod would never forget. But by law, it had been Haim's decision, and the baker had decided to talk with him before deciding his fate.

Haim was a maestro of confectionery, a baker well recognized throughout the kingdom of Pag. The man was also a malgam, which made it a miracle he'd become anything. Part human, and part something else, Haim would typically have been flagged as an unwanted, if not for his gifts.

The old man was pale green, with wispy gray hair that reached his lower back in a long braid. He may have been larger than Clod, but it was hard to tell, as his great shoulders hunched over as if they were too heavy for him to carry. His keen yellow eyes were too small for his head, yet they never missed a stolen cookie or frosting spread too thin. Two thick tusks jutted out from his lower jaw, rising up to his bushy white eyebrows, often making his words hard to understand.

If he'd been a fighter, everyone would've feared him. Fortunately, he was a baker who made delicious, beautiful cakes. People accepted him because of what he could do. Clod liked him because Haim seemed to care.

Clod had never been so scared as the first time he stood alone in the room with Haim. The moment of frivolity with Ada had already left him drowning in guilt. This was a hard-working man taking care of his family, and he didn't deserve the troubles Clod had brought him. He also looked like he could break Clod like a quill.

Haim paced the small room, clenching and unclenching his thumbless hands with nails that could've gutted Clod in a breath. When he finally stopped pacing, Clod stopped breathing.

"How was it?" he asked, his low, resonating voice slurring around the saliva that constantly gathered at his tusks.

"How was wut?" Clod said, choking down his fear. "Uh, sir?"

"The cake," Haim said.

"I…it was…" Clod gulped.

"Say it, boy!" Haim spun around and faced him, growling like an animal.

"That cake was the most delicious thing I ever tasted," Clod said in clipped words.

It was hard to tell, but it looked like the old malgam smiled. "What do you do?" he asked, wiping saliva from his chin.

"Do?" Clod asked.

"We're all magic. You're magic," Haim said, waving a green hand. "Tell me."

Clod was still scared, but that growl made him more frightened of not speaking, so the entire story sort of tumbled out. He told Haim about how the other kids had bullied him, how alone he was until he made Ada. That eventually he learned not to care so much about the bullies since he had a friend, but many still hated him. He explained how Yugen seemed to hate him more than anyone. Finally, he got to the part about the cake, and eating it, and how good it was. Haim nodded for a long time, rubbing those stalagmite tusks growing from his mouth thoughtfully.

"You sculpt," he said.

"Yessir," Clod said.

"If I teach you to sculpt cakes, will you eat them all?"

"Wut?" Clod asked.

"Will you steal my cakes?" Haim asked, articulating each word.

"I promise never to steal again, sir," Clod said. "Even if the cakes are really good."

That almost-smile crept up Haim's cheek once more.

"I want to meet your Ada," he said. "I'll feed you both cake. You learn to sculpt frosting. No more stealing. Three years."

"Yessir," Clod said, staring at the floor.

"Is there anything else, Clod?" the old man asked.

"I…" Clod said.

"Show me respect," Haim said sharply. "Look me in the eye when you speak."

Clod looked the malgam in the eye and saw stern kindness, which filled him with confidence. This man wasn't hateful for someone different. Just the opposite: Haim understood. Looking into his eyes, Clod didn't see Yugen's bitterness, he saw acceptance, and it gave him strength. "I'm sorry, sir. I mean it."

"I believe you," Haim said, setting a heavy hand on Clod's shoulder. "You have tough days ahead, but know that you are forgiven."

Haim hadn't lied. While it wasn't hard labor, like mining or castle-building, it certainly wasn't easy. Hefting flour, stirring vats of batter, delivering enormous cakes without dropping them or eating them. Learning how to be delicate with frosting while forming it into shapes took years.

Haim taught him how to create words, and then flowers, and then people, and then dragons—all with frosting. The baker was far more patient than Yugen, though less patient than his mum. Smacks to the back of his head were sharp without hurting, and pats to his shoulder were more rewarding than any hug. And now, three years later, he could walk away forever. But really, he didn't want to.

A large, familiar hand rested on his shoulder. Haim slurped loudly around his tusks before speaking. "You come back tomorrow, son, and get paid. You have gifts."

"Really?" he asked, looking back at the baker.

The old man nodded, his eyes smiling where his face couldn't. Haim shook his hand firmly, like a gentleman.

"I'd like that," Clod said. "I'll be back after school, sir."

"For your mum and Ada," Haim said, pressing a waxed bag into Clod's hand. He laughed gruffly. "Don't forget to share."

Rain dripped off the wax coating, leaving the delectable contents dry.

"Thank you, sir," Clod said, placing the bag into the pocket of his tunic.

The old malgam nodded and returned to the bakery, closing the door behind him. Large globs of rain pattered the cobblestone road, immediately soaking through his thick rust-colored tunic. The dusky clouds overhead were menacing enough to scare away the sun, making it so dark he didn't see her until she announced herself.

"Tag," Ada said, tapping his leg and scurrying

off.

"Now?" he asked in disbelief.

She didn't stop to answer, so he followed as best he could. Despite the storm, the main road was still busy with gruff-looking wagon drivers and horsemen. Any patience they may have had for a playful teenager was washed away by the poor weather. This was a bad idea, and worry made him clumsy. Clod's shouts for Ada to slow were drowned out by the wet clopping of horse hooves and poorly timed claps of thunder.

It was hard to believe that a sixteen-inch-tall girl of clay could be so nimble. She moved like a fox, dodging between wagon wheels and around ignorant riders who didn't take notice. Clod worried that she would be squished by, well, everything, or even worse, washed away into the gutters.

Despite his concerns, he couldn't hold back the smile. She scurried out of town, scrambling around trees near the path toward their house. Somehow, her tiny legs were faster than his lumbering ones. His heart raced, and he gasped for breath. Running was something other people did, and something he avoided like vegetables.

Clod finally gave into his lost breath, leaning against a tree to catch it. More than anything, he wanted to collapse underneath the canopy of leaves, and hide from the rain. A panic rose in him. Ada would only be here for part of the night, and he would be distraught if she were lost to the woods. He could barely make out a rustle of

41

leaves amidst the pattering of rain. A tiny giggle made his head jerk about. He could just make out her little body peeking from behind nearby brush.

"You're slow," she said, sticking out her tongue.

"Am not," he lied between huffing breaths.

She bolted, and he followed her through a thicket of bushes. Clod immediately knew he should've run around them instead of through as the poky branches tore at his sleeves. He could already hear his mother's sighs. When he finally pushed through the biting branches, they gave way to an open field of shadows. Night would come too soon, and he was antsy to return home, but her laughter egged him on.

Clod slowed to a rush, careful of the dark masses in his path. He didn't know how far they'd run, and wasn't completely sure where they were, but something about this place was eerily familiar. He was haunted by shadows as lightning flashed in the distance, barely enough to feel his way around the cold stone shapes. These weren't natural formations of stone, and he felt a great urgency to leave. He finally stopped, resting against one of the monuments.

"Ada," he called out.

A faint whimper was her only reply, but it was almost impossible to know where it had come from. He stood, still gasping, when a flash of lightning revealed everything. Stone shapes of people surrounded him. That brief flash revealed obscure faces of men and women, each of them posed differently. The lightning was gone, and he had to wonder…had they moved?

"Ada?" he shouted again. "Mum?"

"Clod?" Ada called out, her voice shaky and a little higher than normal.

Careful steps and more shouting led him to the clay girl. He was panting hard when he finally caught up to her, his heart thrumming against his chest like the thick raindrops on the ground. Ada's first reaction was happy panic as she held onto a decorative wrought iron fence, dodging his reaching hand. Even in this disaster of a storm, she still wanted to play.

"Gotcha," Clod said, poking her gently in the stomach. Her laughter lightened his mood, and he gasped out a dull, "Heh."

"What is this place?" she asked, her hand still against the fence.

"I dunno," he said. "But it's scary."

"Maybe it's evil," Ada whispered, peering around at the looming shapes.

Lightning crawled across the low clouds, reaching out like cracks on a shattered window. Clod knelt beside Ada as the statues' heads appeared to move. The lightning had to be tricking his eyes. Please let it be the lightning. Thunder rattled his bones, and they both yelped.

"It's a spell," he said frantically. "It's got to be dark magic!"

They looked at each other and at the same time whispered, "Yugen."

"He's trying to catch us," Clod said. "We need

to get out of here!"

Ada tried pulling away from the fence, her eyes widening with panic. One tiny gray hand was jammed into a leafy iron decoration.

"I'm stuck," she said. "Hurry, before it's too late."

Clod didn't know what to do, worried that too much help may hurt her, so he positioned his giant hands behind her in case she fell. She placed both legs against the leaf and pulled, and tugged, and pulled, until there was a loud snap.

"Ouch," she cried, falling into his hands while grasping her shoulder.

Most of Ada's arm remained stuck in between the black iron leaf and gate spindle, now completely detached from her torso.

"No," Clod said, staring at the arm. This had never happened before. He didn't even think it was possible. She was alive, more or less, and should've been whole for hours.

"Well?" she said hysterically. "Clod, fix it!"

He looked around. There was still no sign of his teacher. Clod pulled Ada close to protect her from the weather, and dug as much of the arm as he could from the fence. His cheeks warmed with embarrassment; he couldn't have felt any clumsier. Picking at it with his finger took too much time, and it was getting harder to see.

"Can you put it back?" Her tiny voice shook.

"Not here," he said. "Let's go home."

Clod didn't run, like during their chase, but his long legs didn't stop once as he found his way to the small cabin. He set Ada near the wood stove, which still gave off a little heat even after their long time away. He lit several candles and placed a log in the stove. She rubbed frantically at her shoulder, her lower lip quivering.

"Does it hurt?" he asked.

"A little," she said. "Why did this happen?"

"I dunno," he said, unable to look her in the eye. He instead focused on rolling the clay remains of her arm between his hands so it was moldable again. "I'll get my tools."

"No! Stop avoiding me," she shouted. "Why did my arm fall off, Clod?"

"I guess I didn't do a very good job," he said, swallowing hard.

Ada began to sob, and each breath that caught was like a stab to his heart. She rarely cried, and never like this. It was a good sign that the arm hadn't turned to ash, and he did his best to warm it with magic. There couldn't be much time, and he hurriedly reconnected it to her shoulder. It was a rushed job, but he wanted her to have an arm and hoped reattaching it would make her stop crying. After several moments of concentration, she could move it again.

Ada's crying slowed to sniffles as she stared at the arm in shock. She looked at him, and then at the arm, lifting it high in the air. Her reattached limb was far longer than it should've been. It was almost horrific, reaching far past her knee.

"Eww," he said. It sort of came out before he could hold it back.

The crying returned, and this time he worried that her little clay tears would wash her face away.

"I'm sorry," he muttered. "Ada, I'm sorry. I didn't mean it. You, uh, you look fine."

"You said eww," she said between gasps, shaking the long appendage in front of her face.

"It won't stay like that, I promise," he pleaded. "When you wake up next time…"

"Now." Sniff. "Now…I'm not just a monster." Sniff. "Now I'm an ugly monster."

"You…you're not a monster," he said. This was almost worse than Ada's arm coming off. He knew how to fix the arm, but was bad at fixing tears. "Who told you that you're a monster?"

"Look at me." She stood. "I've barely grown in five years. I don't look right like you and your mum, and I still only last a day. I see other people, and they're so much more human than you make me. Don't you care anymore?"

"Yuh," he said. "I do care, Ada. I'm sorry. It's just hard. I guess I'm not as good at sculpting as my dad, and if I use more clay it makes me tired."

"What about all the pretty things you make with frosting?" Ada asked.

"Well, that's different," he said. "It's easy."

"So, you're being lazy?" she asked, her eyes wide.

"Yuh," he said, knowing she was right. He wished he could go back and try harder, but it was too late for that. "I guess I am."

"Then don't bring me back," she said.

"Ada, no," he said. "Don't say that."

"Friendship takes a lot of work, Clod. You have to try, you have to care, even when it's hard," she said, the disappointment in her voice even more crushing than the look on her face. "I don't want to look like a child, anymore. I want to be bigger, and I believe you can do it. You can do anything, Clod, but you have to try. Friendship…life is about give and take. Sometimes you have to give, and you need to start giving me more."

"I promise," he said. "I'll do better."

He sat cross-legged with his elbows against his knees and his chin resting on his hands. Balancing life between school and working at the bakery was exhausting. When it finally came time for Ada to wake, Clod had been doing what was familiar. It was fast, but at least they got to spend time together. He hadn't thought to ask her what she wanted.

Long moments passed until he finally muttered, "I still don't think you're ugly. I think you're beautiful."

Ada abruptly made a loud honking sound, sort of hunched over, holding her too-long arm against her face. She lumbered over to him slowly, letting the arm rock back and forth, her hand dragging across the floor like a broom. It was the weirdest thing he'd ever seen, and he couldn't hold back a smile.

"I'm a beautiful elephant," she said in a goofy voice. She stopped long enough to make another honking noise.

He barked out a low laugh, and she giggled. It became contagious. Their laughter broke through his melancholy, but didn't completely wash away the guilt.

"Do you still want to come back, Ada?" he asked.

"Of course I do," she said, rolling her eyes. "You'd be boring without me."

"Good," he said. "I'm sorry."

"Just…just try harder," she said. "Please."

"I'll make you the most beautiful elephant ever," he said with a smirk.

"What?" she said, jumping onto his chest.

He rolled back as if she'd actually knocked him over, making him laugh again. The cottage door opened, and his mum entered with a bag of food.

"You two." She shook her head with a look of disbelief that quickly became a frown. "Ada, what happened to your arm, dear?"

Ada and Clod proceeded to talk over each other excitedly as they recounted their adventure. Eidy smiled and nodded as she hustled about the small room preparing dinner. When Clod told her about the statues, she stopped what she was doing and stared. He reached into his pocket and pulled out the waxed bag of treats from the bakery. "And I brought dessert."

"You were where?" she said, her voice stern enough to make them both rear back. When she turned to look at them, her face had gone pale, and she set a pan on the table.

"Some place with a bunch of statues," Clod said, trying his best not to make it a big deal.

"And Master Learned Yugen was casting evil spells to make it scary," Ada said, nodding vigorously. "But we got away in time."

Something about that place nagged at his memories like hovering fruit flies. "Where were we? Was that a graveyard?"

"I told you not to go to there," his mum shouted.

Clod dropped the bag. He'd never seen such fury in her eyes. They made her seem both angry and frightened. Almost as frightened as he was. She may have been smaller, but she was still his mum.

"I'm sorry," he said, swallowing hard. "I didn't know we were *there*."

"I led him through the woods. It was my fault," Ada said, trying to cross her arms. The long one flopped to the floor.

"No, it was mine," Clod said. "I wasn't paying attention."

"Tell me what you saw," Eidy said.

"Just scary stone faces in the lightning," Clod said, suddenly shivering from being so wet. Something long and cold brushed his cheek, and he jumped back. "Ahh!"

"Gotcha," Ada said, pulling her arm away with a laugh. "I bet you won't be messing up my arm again."

"Not when you're an elephant," he said, sticking out his tongue.

She reached for him with the long arm, and he pulled back again, making her laugh.

"Clod, Ada," his mum snapped.

They both stopped and faced her.

"I want you to promise me you won't go back," she said in a tone of forced calm. She wasn't smiling, not even a little.

"But why?" he asked. "It was just a—"

"If I learn that you go back there—and I will find out. I'm your mum—I won't bring you clay for a year!"

"What?" Ada asked.

"You can't do that," Clod said, standing up.

"I can, and I will," his mum said.

His heart raced more than it had in the woods. "I'll...I'll get my own clay...and..."

"Go to your room, Clod," she said, pointing.

"Fine," he said. "Come on, Ada."

"No," his mum said. "Ada and I are going to have a little talk. You go in there and think about what I said."

"But...but she won't be here for much longer," Clod said, now very worried.

"You'll see her in two weeks." Her tone was cold, and bore the finality of a locked door made of solid steel. She pointed to the other room. "Now!"

Clod couldn't have moved slower as each labored step brought him to the room. He braved a final glance at Ada, whose hands shook with the same fright he was feeling. The bedroom was dark, and despite his great size, it took several nudges to close the door. He collapsed onto his pallet, feeling completely hopeless. He tried listening, but could only hear mutters, and gasps, and crying. And then the talking stopped, and Clod knew that Ada was gone. She was ash again, and he hadn't been there to say goodbye.

An hour passed before his mum finally called to him. "You can come out for dinner."

"Not hungry," Clod said. He'd never been so angry at his mum. Tomorrow, he would leave, and go somewhere where he could find his own clay. They would be far away from Yugen. And when he molded Ada, she would be taller than ever. He could do it, and nobody could stop him, and one day, she wouldn't leave him ever again.

And these tearful thoughts of his mean mum, and Master Learned Yugen, and his dear Ada followed Clod into sleep and beyond.

Age 16

"Sometimes, we find a diamond in the rough, Eidy," Headmaster Yugen said with a long sigh. "And other times, we are stuck with coal."

"What?" his mother said in the angry voice that made Clod wince.

"If he has no magic, he's nothing more than his name," Yugen said. "Does he have magic?"

"I…" she said, her words trailing off. "No."

"You're a liar, and your son is a thief," Yugen said. "What else did he learn from you?"

"I'm not a liar," she pleaded. "You're making us sound evil."

"I know about her," he said.

His mum gasped and stumbled over her words before composing herself. "Fine, you're right, he made her. But, since he has magic, doesn't that mean you can teach him?"

"It's not magic I recognize, and I've chosen to overlook that disgusting aberration because your son is too dull to do anything dangerous," Yugen said. "But I can't let it go any further. I've notified the Council of Elders that Clod can do magic even I cannot sense. That means it can only come from the dark. My advice to you is to make him stop before his soul is corrupted…if it's not already too late."

His mother began to cry. She didn't deserve this, and hiding under Yugen's window, listening like a sneak-thief, made Clod feel like a coward. Even as he balled up his shaking fists and planted them into the ground, Ada rested a calming hand on his.

"They'll hear you," she warned. "Don't make this worse for her."

"Quit being so smart all the time," he said.

"Quit acting like you're dumb," she snapped, her light-brown brows furrowing. "Now shush, I can't hear them."

"Just because you can't sense it doesn't mean it's evil," Eidy said. "Can't you teach him to use his magic differently?"

"It doesn't work that way," Yugen said softly, almost as if he cared. "If I could, I would imbue all these children with great power to do good. Most of them are musical instruments that I tune throughout their youth. The type of magic a person can cast is typically passed down generation to generation. If I can't recognize his abilities, and you have no magic to pass down, then it must come from darkness. Unless you're lying again?"

"No," his mum said weakly.

"See," Yugen said in a winning tone. "Evil is a disease that spreads like infection. Only the most powerful, like the learned, can avoid its taint. I advise that he avoids temptation and concentrates on a future of physical labor. He should make the most of his life now, since he'll probably die at a young age, like his father."

Ada stood and began crawling up him toward the window, grumbling curses. It was okay for him, or Ada, to ask about his dad, but only barely. Clod had stopped asking when he was old enough to realize his mum would save the tears until after she thought he was asleep. There'd been a lot of love, and a final gift, and then his dad was gone. Clod had wanted to know more, but was told to wait until he was older. He respected his mum enough to be patient.

He'd also kept his promise not to clobber Yugen. Ada wasn't so restrained, and he bear-hugged her until she stopped trying to climb through the window.

"What do you suggest?" Eidy asked, a coldness to her voice.

"Clod is a sizable lad," Yugen said. "With some initiative, he would be ideal for mining, or—"

"But," Eidy interrupted. "But what about the bakery? What about his sculpting? His father was an artist."

"Baker Haim, that malgam, is too kind. I've seen that thing your son created," Yugen said, his words dripping with sneer.

"Ada," his mother said, almost whispering.

"Right," Yugen replied as if she'd provided a bad excuse for turning in homework late. "I presume that creature is one of his sculptures."

"Yes."

Yugen's laugh sounded like a turkey being choked. "Apparently your Clod can't sculpt anything that looks better than a clod of dirt," he said between turkey-laughs. When he finally calmed down, he stated with a certain finality, "He isn't that good, is he?"

His mother didn't reply, which made Clod angry all over again. Ada looked, well, like Ada. She was still, mostly, the color of muddy clay, but she had eyes now instead of empty holes. She could smile, with teeth, and had all her fingers. She was also taller, more than two feet. He could've done a better job with more time. That was his greatest challenge. He was still in school, and worked in Haim's bakery. Clod had a choice. Either bring Ada to life every other week, or spend more time adding finer detail to make her appear more human. So, really, he didn't have a choice. He'd be alone without her.

"I like how I look," she said with a disgruntled frown. "I can tell how hard you try."

"Not good enough. I can do better," he whispered. "But it would take longer, and I'd miss you."

"I just want to be taller," she said.

"I know," he said. "I'll figure out how."

She approved with a nod before leaning to the

window once more. The school didn't allow much opportunity for sneaking, as though it was designed that way. He'd been surprised the window was cracked open just enough for them to hear. It was as if Yugen had done so on purpose, knowing Clod would listen in, but wouldn't be able to do anything without getting in trouble.

"You are my last conference for the day, and I believe everything has been covered," he said abruptly. "Did you have any other questions?"

"None," Eidy said, her tone crisp as the first frost of fall.

"Clod is sixteen now, and almost a young man," Yugen said. "He is welcome to stay in school, but I strongly advise that you begin seeking a viable future for him before it is too late."

"I understand," she said. His mother sounded so defeated.

"You're welcome, Eidy," he said, even though she hadn't thanked him. "Let me know if I can provide your son with a pick or a shovel."

How was it possible for a demonfart like Yugen to keep getting promoted? He didn't deserve to be headmaster. Clod wanted to leap through the window and beat his principal in the face. Ada tugged at his sleeve, and he reluctantly followed. They crawled away from the school window until it was out of sight and scurried to the nearby woods. Clod picked up a rock and threw it at a tree. It bounced off and hit him in the cheek, which sent Ada into a fit of laughter. It stung, a lot, and even her laugh couldn't keep him from being angry.

"I don't want to fix roads or make buildings," he said. "I sculpt. I've got magic."

"Why don't they like your magic?" she asked. "I do."

"I don't know," he said, glaring at his feet. "Nobody will tell me. The other kids say I'm a freak, and Mum says don't worry about it."

"I think you'll be an amazing sculptor," Ada said.

"Yeah?" he asked, looking up at her.

"Haim likes what you do at the bakery," she said.

"Haim likes me a lot more than Yugen," Clod agreed with a nod. "But that doesn't mean I'm good."

"Look at me now," she said, holding her arms out and spinning around. "I have fingers, and toes, and eyes, and even eyebrows." Ada raised and lowered her eyebrows comically.

"I'm trying," he said, unable to hold back his frustration. "It takes so long to collect so much clay, now that I know where Mum was getting it. Sometimes I have to do it at night when the other kids aren't waiting to make fun of me. By the time I have enough, I only have a few days to finish you up."

"Maybe if you show me how, I can help," she prodded.

"Really?" he asked. "I hadn't thought of that. We can go try right now. Do we have time?"

She squeezed her eyes shut and concentrated.

After several moments, she shook her head. "Nope. Maybe an hour left."

This day was awful, and the disappointment in her face matched how he felt.

"Well, it's a great idea," he said.

"Next time," she said, her voice filled with encouragement. "I'm lasting longer though. I can almost last a day and a half."

"Yeah," he said, kicking at some leaves.

"So," Ada said with a hint of mischief in her voice. "What now? More rock throwing?"

"No," he replied, dropping the rock he'd just picked up. "Maybe...I just wish I could teach Yugen a lesson, that's all. He doesn't really want to teach. He just wants to feel more important. Now he's headmaster in charge of the whole school. I wish there was a way we could make him feel as bad as he made my mum feel."

She placed a finger on her cheek and tapped thoughtfully. The dark pupil in the middle of her gray eyeballs moved from side to side, and Clod knew what that meant.

"You're going to get me in trouble again," he said, feeling a little worried.

"It's better than pouting," she said, "or throwing rocks at yourself."

"Yeah," he said, rubbing his cheek. Rocks and trees were stupid, but Ada's ideas weren't. The rewards always outweighed the risks, and he was unable to hold back a smile. "What are we going to do?"

"Do you know where Yugen goes after

school?" she asked.

"He always rides slowly through town on that dumb horse before going to the same dumb pub," Clod said, frowning.

"We need to go there," she said.

"But how?" he asked. "People will see you! Mum says we could get in big trouble."

"I need a jacket," she said quickly. "And a hat."

"Okay, but we need to hurry," Clod said. "You don't have much time."

They ran through the woods, jumping over fallen branches, and ducking under living ones. She laughed as they rushed through a patch of wildflowers, dragging her hands across the tops. Bees and butterflies scattered in dismay. He felt so alive, and so very happy that they were up to something.

When they arrived at his empty home, he was out of breath, but too excited to let that stop him. Clod grabbed a ragged coat and an old red hat with a wide brim that his mum sometimes wore when gardening. The hat was much too big for Ada, but successfully covered her face. Even after rolling up the sleeves, the jacket looked like she was wearing hand-me-downs from a giant sibling.

"How do I look?" she asked.

He could barely make out her smile beneath the brim's shadow.

"Who are you?" he asked.

"What?" she asked. "Clod, it's me, Ada."

"I know," he said with a chuckle. "It just

doesn't look like you. You look like a little person."

"I am a little person," she said, placing her hand on her hips. "Aren't I?"

"Yeah," he said, still gasping for breath from their run. "My favorite little person."

She gave him a hug before they hurried out the door. Town was too far away. Even this short, she was still faster than him. Maybe he should make her legs even shorter. They held hands as they rushed along the rocky path. He really wanted to know what she was planning, but was too busy gasping to ask. When the winding path from his cottage met cobblestone, they slowed to a brisk walk.

Worry struck him that someone would see Ada. Would they say something? Would they try to destroy her? The sidewalk alongside the road was crowded with people going places, and Clod soon realized that nobody took note of them. They were just two kids, walking together, amongst the crowd. His mother had told him never to come to town with Ada again, and he was giddy with the realization that they were doing it anyway.

"Don't go all the way to the pub," she said. "Just most of the way."

"Almost there," he said.

"Hopefully we aren't too late," she said, rubbing her tiny hands together.

They stopped in front of a curio shop and watched the road. His anticipation grew with every minute that passed, and cool sweat beaded down his cheeks. Ada only had moments before going away, and he wondered if she would be here long enough to see out her plan.

"There," he said, pointing.

She tugged at his sleeve, pulling his hand down. Headmaster Yugen rode a tall black stallion, easily eighteen hands high and nearly as proud as his rider. The horse trotted pretentiously along the road. Yugen's head was raised high as he looked down his long nose at everyone. He ignored most who waved politely, nodding only at a few.

Ada pulled Clod in close so she could whisper. "Do you remember how Yugen said you weren't very good at sculpting?"

"Yeah," Clod said.

"That means he doesn't think I look like a real person, right?" she asked, handing over the hat.

"He's a jerk," Clod said, defensively.

"Promise me you'll wait here," she said, her eyes wide with excitement. "Promise."

"I promise," he said.

"I mean it," she said, letting go of his hand. "I'll be okay."

"I said I promise," he said sharply.

She kissed him on the cheek and ran out to the middle of the road. Yugen was far too distracted nodding at someone with his nose. Despite gasps and warnings from onlookers, he hadn't noticed Ada standing in front of his horse until it was too late. Clod watched in horror as the stallion trampled his best friend. Hooves dug into her mercilessly, crushing Ada into the stone road.

Clod didn't know what to do. It had happened so fast, he hadn't had time to stop her. She couldn't be hurt, much. At least, he didn't think she could. He'd promised to stay put, but hadn't realized she was going to be crushed by a horse. Before he could rush forward, cries from the crowd caught Yugen's attention.

"No," Yugen cried, pulling hard on the reins of his stallion. "Hold!"

The horse stopped, and Yugen leaped off. A mob of people moved forward, their growing anger palpable. It had looked like Yugen's horse had trampled a young girl because he was too busy being important to pay attention. Even as he drew his mount off the mangled coat, the angry mob began shouting and shoving. The principal looked nervous, his pale face white as snow. Soldiers rushed over, staring him down sternly as they formed a circle around the damage he'd wrought.

Dropping to his knees, Yugen tried lifting Ada from the pavement. "A healer," he called out. "By the gods, this body doesn't feel right. I need a healer."

The crowd of gasps and cries moved closer as Yugen turned her over.

"I'm so sorry child, I'm so…" His eyes went wide.

"Gotcha," Ada wheezed with a smile before falling to ash in his arms. Yugen abruptly stood, jerking the coat from the ground, surrounded by a cloud of gray dust.

The crowd went silent. Some were angry, others furious, and most confused. All of them stared accusingly at Yugen. She was right. If he'd been such a bad sculptor, nobody would've cared. Best friend ever.

Yugen took a deep breath, and yelled, "Cloooood!"

One soldier grabbed him by the arm roughly, jerking the coat from his hands. Ash blew in the breeze, making both soldiers look around quizzically.

"Where's the kid?" one of them asked Yugen.

"She's not a kid," he said. "She was a sculpture."

"Riiight," the guard replied in disbelief. "What kind of magic would make a girl turn to dust after trampling her with a horse? You always taught me that dark magic was bad."

"Me too," said the other man, taking the reins of the horse. "Before failing me out of school."

"This wasn't *my* dark magic! It's impossible for me to be infected," Yugen shouted, looking around desperately until his eyes fell on Clod. "Him. Ask that boy. Clod, tell him this was just your sculpture."

"I'm pretty sure I couldn't sculpt anything that looked better than a clod of dirt," Clod. "Headmaster Learn-ed Yugen."

Yugen's eyes went wide, his pale cheeks becoming a deeper shade of red with every angry huff of breath.

"Clod?" a soldier asked. "Haim's apprentice?"

"I'm working tomorrow, sir," Clod said. "Please stop by if you want some cakes. On the house for keeping us safe."

"See you tomorrow, then," the man replied before turning to Yugen. "A few hours in the stocks should calm you down."

"Didn't he say you should dig ditches?" said the other soldier.

"That's right," he replied. "I hope nobody forgets he's locked up. That would make for a long night."

"Tell them, boy," Yugen shouted. "Tell them the truth, or..."

The soldier grabbed the back of Yugen's thin neck, and his headmaster went quiet. Most of the crowd followed in awe, but Clod couldn't. He was laughing so hard, he had to sit down.

Age 17

"You have to do it, Clod," Ada said, her tone pleading. "Just look at him."

"But…but I…" he said, choosing to avoid the child and instead looking into his friend's eyes.

"Please," she said, tugging at his hand and pointing. "Look at him."

They'd joined a crowd surrounding a small boy of nine or ten. He was holding the body of a puppy who'd lost a brief battle with a team of horses. Several onlookers had been too slow to catch the speedy little dog, including Clod and Ada.

"She jumped from my arms when she saw the horse," the boy said through sobs, his teary eyes glancing up at a woman who gently patted his head.

"I'm sorry, child," a woman said. "This happens sometimes. Maybe your parents could buy you a new puppy."

"But Lady was *my* puppy!" The boy shook his head. "I didn't even get to say goodbye."

"You have to," Ada said firmly, tugging at his sleeve.

"But I don't know what will happen," Clod said. "I could make it worse. I always make it worse."

"You always make me better," she said hurriedly. "What are you worried about?"

"The dog may be hurt or lame if I try," he said, his mind reeling with fear.

"You make me whole, and I'm nothing but clay," she said softly. "The dog is made of bones and flesh."

"You're a lot more than clay," he said, unable to shake his worry.

"Clod, are you being selfish?" she asked.

Ada had struck a nerve. He only got to spend two days with her every other week, and even though she helped him collect clay, it took a lot out of him to will her to life. It was especially hard now that she was almost three feet tall. He really needed this time with her. The last week had been particularly tough. Yugen had failed him on an exam he knew he'd passed, and he'd been pushed into the mud by the bullies. Twice. He could've beaten up the bullies, and evil Yugen, for that matter, but had promised his mum not to. This week hated him, and it was about to get worse.

"A little selfish," he admitted, looking at the ground. "I don't think I can bring the dog back, and keep you alive at the same time."

"Dear Clod," she said. "You are sweet to want to keep me, but this child needs you, and I'll be back soon."

"How can I fix...that?" he said, pointing at the mess of a pup.

"You can do more than you believe," she said softly.

"I can?" he asked.

She pulled him down and kissed his cheek, which made him smile wide enough to show his jagged teeth. Something he never did.

"Okay," he said. "I'll do it."

"Thank you, Clod," she said, clasping her hands together and looking at the corpse.

Clod knelt beside the child and gently placed a hand on the dog's tiny head. He willed, with every fiber in his being, he willed and concentrated until sweat dripped from his cheeks. This was so much harder than bringing Ada back; he wasn't completely sure he could. But she'd been certain, and that was enough.

He was tired, and his heart thrummed painfully in his chest. Ada gasped, collapsing behind him, and he knew it was done. The dog yipped, the child squealed, and the crowd muttered as it collectively moved away.

"What's your name?" Clod asked, gasping for breath.

"Michael," the child said, sobbing and smiling at the same time. "Thank you."

"You may not want to thank me yet," Clod began. "My magic will only bring her back for a short while. Maybe a day. Long enough for you to say goodbye."

"Oh?" the boy said, his chin quivering.

"Give Lady the best day of her life," Clod said. "It will be a better way to go, for both of you."

"I will," Michael said, smiling as Lady licked his face. "I promise."

"Ouch," Clod called as he was dragged up by an ear.

"What have you done?" Headmaster Yugen spat as he jerked Clod about.

"I wanted to help," he said.

"The only thing you've done is create another abomination," he shouted. "Nothing good will come of this!"

Ada was a pile of ash, as he'd feared, but the look on Michael's face had been worth it. The child was all smiles, from his cheeks to his eyes.

"You'll get the best day, Lady," Michael said. "We'll chase squirrels, and birds, and butterflies. I'll ask Mom to make you the best dinner. And then you can rest." The words were strained from heartache, but the sentiment was full of love and happiness.

"Looks like I've created some good, too," Clod said defiantly.

"Thank you," Michael said to Clod before scrambling off.

"Follow them," Yugen said to one of the bruisers beside him. He let go of Clod's ear and grasped his arm. "Don't interfere. If it becomes a monster, kill it again."

"Leave them alone!" Clod thundered.

The man nodded once before pushing his way through the crowd. Yugen waved the mob off as if swatting at bees. Most of the bees leered at Clod suspiciously, but several nodded in appreciation. The woman who'd been consoling the boy patted Clod on the chest before leaving.

"Why do you hate me so much?" Clod asked, jerking his arm away. It stung to free it from the principal's firm grip. Yugen was smaller than him, but his fingers had tightened painfully like a vise.

"I don't hate you," Yugen said coolly. "I hate what you do. There is already too much dark magic in this world, and yours is the darkest. It is evil, and ugly, and will not be allowed."

"How can that be evil?" Clod asked, pointing to the boy running down the street. "How can Ada be evil?"

"Foolish child," he said. "What you don't know makes you even more dangerous. Now come with me."

* * * *

Clod had never felt so frightened, and desperately wished Ada were here with him. The Council of Elders rarely gathered at the town hall, and only for the most heinous of crimes. Seven of the eight seats were filled on the high bench, looking down at him sternly with wizened eyes.

Shaman Millow sat on the far left, her black face sweaty and shoulders broad with enough strength to break him. Beside her sat Monk Syt, hiding beneath dark purple robes, her long yellow fangs shining dully in the candlelight. Cleric Dyes was the definition of stern, from his tight brown beard to his crisp gray robes. Priest Muane sat in the center. He had to be 200 years old, with a long, long white beard and a skullcap that covered his baldness. Wizard Pyle sat to the right of Muane. Everything about the man appeared gentle, from his long, soft, white beard to his tired blue eyes. There was an empty seat beside Pyle. Next to that empty seat was a woman who made Clod blush. Caine the Magician had big, blond hair that poured over a lot of tanned skin. She was beautiful in a sultry way that made his mother nudge him any time he stared. Hetomancer Styff could've been the librarian in his school, and he felt shushed every time he looked at her.

It wasn't just the elders that made this council so frightening. The Great Chamber was an enormous, empty room that could've held three of his houses. It was round, with a domed ceiling that had people painted on it—all of them glaring down in judgment. Everything was white stone, from ceiling to floor and high bench to stairs. It was a cold, stark place filled with staring eyes. In all his life, he'd never felt so small. Ada must have felt like this all the time, and he mentally kicked himself for not making her taller. For a moment, he wondered if he was tiny enough in this great place to scurry away, like a mouse, but the moment passed quickly. They would notice, all of them.

His mother and Yugen were the only other people in the room beside the council. There was no need for guards. The seven seated at the high bench held enough power to decimate armies. Despite this, his mother looked fierce. Every time she glanced at him, her eyes were filled with love and understanding. Those eyes would then glare at the seven with a stern defiance that shook him to his core.

Yugen, on the other hand, rubbed his hands together hungrily, as if his due was finally coming. "As I've told the council, the clutch of dark magic has grasped more of my students than I've ever seen," he said. "Too many have been lured by its power."

"Too many of your students, Yugen," Caine agreed. "And do you believe it is this teenager who draws them into the dark?"

"Clod?" he said with a laugh. "No. I'm surprised this fool can put on his own shoes. This is exactly why he's a threat, because he is dense and holds dangerous, dark power that even I cannot sense. As I have promised the council, I will bring purveyors of any dark magic I find to justice, and—"

"Ms. Eidy," Priest Muane interrupted, his voice low and calm. "How long have you known your son could bring back the dead?"

"I didn't realize..." she said, looking distraught. "He creates a clay figure that he plays with. His magic makes her talk and move."

"I see." The old priest lowered his head, looking at Principal Yugen with a concerned gaze. "You fear a student who makes a homunculus?"

"An aberration," Yugen spat.

"How long has he been able to create this creature?" Millow, the Shaman of Ester, asked.

"Her name is Ada," Clod muttered. "And she's my friend, not a creature."

Nine heads all turned to him as if suddenly struck with the realization that, not only was he in the room, he could speak words.

"So, you call your homunculus Ada?" Wizard Pyle said, his tone as gentle as the expression on his face.

"She told me that's her name," he said.

"She...told...you?" the old wizard said as if the words didn't go together.

His mother looked at him with eyes pleading for him to stop, but something about the wizard made him relax, and trust. Pyle seemed to care, albeit a little.

"Yes, during her first visit," Clod said.

"I don't understand," Shaman Millow said. "You said she comes to visit, but I thought you made her out of clay."

"I do make her out of clay," Clod said. "And then she visits."

"It sounds like a homunculus to me," Cleric Dyes said sternly.

AGE 17

"Except that homunculi don't give themselves names," Wizard Pyle said, pinching at his short, dark beard.

"Could this be demonology?" Millow asked and was immediately answered with shrugs. "Clod. Has Ada ever done anything to harm you? Has she ever caused mischief?"

Principal Yugen clucked his tongue loudly. He stood tall and took a deep breath of pride before glaring down at Clod long enough to make the teenager gulp. "They are always causing mischief."

"In what way?" Millow asked. "Are they drinking the blood of hens? Have they sacrificed any small rodents in circles of fire?"

"Ewww," Clod said. That was disgusting. The Shaman had to be making it up.

She arched an eyebrow at him, her face contorted in surprise. "Apparently not," Millow said. "Well, Yugen?"

Yugen coughed into a hand, blushing slightly before he explained some of the more creative pranks Clod and Ada had pulled, including the time Ada had walked in front of his horse.

His mother's eyes were wide, her face torn between shock and anger. The more pranks Yugen described, the more idiotic Clod appeared and the more heated her expression became. He blurted out a nervous chuckle that made heads turn once again. For the briefest of moments, it looked like Shaman Millow smiled.

"This doesn't sound like demonology," Muane

said. "It sounds a bit more like pranks. This can't be the first lark you have experienced in the classroom, Yugen."

"My students respect me," Yugen said, his face stoic.

"We do?" Clod asked, looking at him in disbelief. He was going to say more until his mother placed a hand on his shoulder.

Several of the elders laughed, and Yugen's cheeks flushed a darker shade of red.

"Child," the wizard said, "have you brought anything else back to life?"

"No, sir," Clod said. "I sort of didn't want to bring the puppy back because I thought it would make Ada go away, but she insisted."

"Oh?" Millow asked.

"I didn't want to. I was afraid if I woke the boy's pup, she would go away. I only get to see her once every two weeks, but she was right," Clod said. "I was being selfish. So, I helped the puppy so that boy could say goodbye. That's why Ada isn't here."

"You can only animate one at a time?" Wizard Pyle asked.

"I guess," Clod said. He felt helpless. It was impossible to explain something he just did. How could one explain breathing or listening?

"Do you think you could bring back something larger?" Muane asked.

Clod shrugged. "I can only make Ada this tall," he said, holding his hand up to approximate Ada's height.

The council members looked at each other, matching nods and smiles.

"Have you ever taken a life?" Styff asked coldly.

"I chased a mouse out of our home one winter," Clod said, reeling from guilt. "I felt bad because it was cold out, but mum wouldn't get off the chair until it was gone."

Eidy looked down, blushing furiously, while the council chuckled once more.

"Yugen," Wizard Pyle said. "What have you done to cultivate this gift?"

"What?" Yugen asked, his tone sharp. "I've been trying to suppress it. I couldn't sense his magic, which means it has to be evil."

"There is nothing evil with infusing your life into something or someone else," Cleric Dyes said. "Clod may not understand, but there is a cost in doing so. Even if it merely tires him, it's a selfless act."

"Very selfless," Monk Syt said. "He gave up time with his friend to help another."

Shaman Millow stood and walked down the stone steps to approached Clod and his mum. "You did a good thing, helping that boy, Clod. Please be careful whom you help. There are some who would take advantage of what you can do. Do you understand?"

He didn't, completely, but nodded anyway.

"I would like to visit you at your home one day," she said to his mum. "To meet Ada, and talk about Clod."

"You would be most welcome," Eidy said, with a respectful bow of her head.

"Thank you for your time," Wizard Pyle said. "You are free to leave while we discuss teaching methods with Learn-ed Yugen."

"Headmaster," Yugen corrected with a polite cough.

"No," Millow said. "I believe Learn-ed is a more appropriate title."

Yugen shot a glare at Clod that almost knocked him over. Even though he'd wanted his teacher to be in trouble, something about that look scared him.

"Let's go," his mum said, pulling him out by his arm.

"Am I in trouble?" he whispered.

"You probably should be," she said. "You've caused a lot of mischief, but I'm proud of what you did for that boy."

"But what about the evil?" he asked.

His mum stopped before they'd exited the hall and turned to face him. Her eyes were as serious and determined as he'd ever seen. "Everyone has power, Clod. Everyone. Most cast spells, some use muscle, others use words. The difference between good and evil is what you decide to do with that power."

"So, I'm not evil?" he asked.

"Like I said," she replied. "That's for you to decide."

Age 19

"Shaman Millow," his mum said from the front room. Her voice shook with each word. "How...how can I help you? Is something wrong?"

"Get ready to run for it," Clod whispered to Ada from behind his hand.

"There will be no running, young man," the sharp voice of the shaman said. "And no need for it."

Ada's wide eyes and dropped jaw mirrored his own, and he carefully peeked around the door frame. The solid figure of old Shaman Millow was already a step past the entrance. She appeared more tired than he remembered, haggard even. Her black hair was the huge windblown mess of someone who didn't care, or didn't have time to care. She was much shorter than Clod, and she leaned on a gnarled wooden staff, but her presence was formidable.

It wasn't just her magic, which was great beyond myths and legends. Millow was broad of shoulder with strong hands that gripped the staff with a fierce strength. She filled her robes, but didn't appear overweight. Simply put, the woman was built like a wall. Piercing blue eyes, wise as the years were long, peered from her dark face. He didn't feel fear, merely the respect you would show when crossing paths with a wild bear in the woods.

"Come here, Clod," she said, waving him over with a meaty hand. "And your friend, too. It took longer than I intended, but I came to see you both."

Clod took careful steps into the room. Ada grasped two of his thick fingers with a death grip. They stopped, just beyond arm's reach, as if that was enough space to keep them safe from a force of nature.

"My, you're much taller than I remember," she said, reaching out to shake his hand.

He didn't know what to do, so nervous that his hand was quivering. He looked to his mother, who nodded, her eyes wide. With a deep breath, he took Millow's work-worn hand and was immediately grateful he didn't explode.

"Grip harder, son," Millow said. "You're a man now, and you won't hurt me."

"Yes, ma'am," he said, gripping as firmly as he dared. No one had ever told him how to shake hands. Clod always felt it was necessary to be overly gentle. The last thing he wanted was to hurt anyone.

She nodded once before letting go. "Please, call me Shaman Millow, or just shaman."

"Okay," he said. The way she said it, shaman sounded kind of like grandma. Something about that made him relax.

Millow leaned slightly to one side, peering around Clod. Ada was now behind him, gripping his sleeve and trembling.

"I don't want to go," Ada said, her voice quiet.

"I won't let her take you," Clod said. "I promise."

"I'm scared, Clod," Ada said.

Clod stood to his full height and faced Shaman Millow. "Are you here to make her go away?"

"I don't understand?" Millow asked, looking quizzically at Eidy.

"Yugen kicked Clod out of school last year and said one day, someone would make Ada go away forever," Eidy said. "Because she's made from evil."

"I see." Millow sighed, shaking her head. "Ada, how many live bats have you eaten this month?"

"Ewww," Ada said. "None."

"Demons," Millow snapped. "Tell me now, how many demons have you summoned today?"

"None," Ada said, stepping out from behind Clod's leg. "What's a demon?"

"At dawn's first light," Millow said, lowering her face until it was covered in ominous shadow, "did you go naked into the woods, draw your own blood over fire, and swear your soul to Abbrasis the Cursed?"

"I woke up early," Ada said with wide eyes. "But I couldn't sleep because of Clod's snoring, and he's too big for me to roll over."

"Sorry," Clod muttered.

"What did you do?" Millow asked.

"I went outside to pick flowers," she said, pointing at a wooden cup filled with dandelions.

"You certainly don't sound like the source of all evil in this land," Shaman Millow said, winking at Eidy.

"I'm not!" Ada stomped a little foot and crossed her arms.

"Then I'm not going to make you go anywhere you don't wish to go," Millow said, clearing her throat to cover a chuckle.

"Promise?" Clod asked.

"By the elements, I swear if Ada is not evil then I shall not banish her," Millow said sincerely. "As long as I can have some tea."

"Oh," his mother said. "I...I'm sorry, Shaman Millow. I have clean water, but no tea."

"That's all right, dear," Millow said gently, patting Eidy's hand. "Please bring me a pot of water and four cups."

His mother took a pot and rushed outside. She returned moments later with a strained expression, water dripping out of the pot, and a wet apron.

"Just place it on the stove," Millow said, making her way across the small room.

"I can get some wood," Clod offered.

Millow shook her head as she waved a hand over the stove. Fire, without wood, burned hot within the iron. She reached into a pouch hanging from her belt and sprinkled the contents over the pot, which was boiling by the time she was done. Leaning over it, Millow sniffed deeply and nodded.

"This will be a bit sweeter than the tea you're used to," she said.

"Well," his mother said, biting her lip. "We're used to water, so I'm sure it will be."

Millow laughed, and tension seemed to clear like a fog lifting.

"Would you like to sit while I serve the tea?" Eidy asked. Her hands shook as she looked nervously at the magical fire. "I'm sorry, there's only one chair. We don't really have much."

"It looks to me like you have everything you need," the shaman said, appraising the room with an appreciative smile. "Your home reminds me of my own, more or less."

"Really?" Clod asked.

"I have two chairs," she allowed. Millow sat on the floor and crossed her legs, placing her staff on top of them.

Eidy handed her a wooden cup filled with the tea, which she sipped noisily. His mum held the next cup to her nose, sniffed it several times, eyed it suspiciously, and then drank.

"Yum," she said, and nodded to Clod as she handed it over. "You'll like this."

"If you say so," he said half-heartedly. He took the cup from his mother and sipped the tiniest amount he could. Sugary goodness warmed him, and he sat on the floor before Shaman Millow. This wasn't the bitter earthy taste of the tea his mother brought home on a rare occasion. That tea reminded him of vegetables. This tea reminded him of Haim's bakery, and he wondered if there would be enough for a second cup even before finishing the first.

Ada eyed the cup she'd been handed with the caution of a puppy walking through snow for the first time. Shaman Millow lowered her tea and watched, one long eyebrow rising curiously. Ada's little gray tongue dipped carefully into the hot beverage. She mouthed the flavor with a smack and her eyes went wide. Her deep gulp of hot tea was immediately followed by panting. Clod wouldn't have been surprised to see steam rise from her mouth and ears.

"It'th hot," she said, waving air at her lolling tongue.

"You drink," Millow observed.

"When I'm thirsty," Ada replied with a gentle frown.

"Of course," Millow said. "But I thought you were made of clay."

"She's made from clay," Clod corrected.

"Please come here…uh…child," Millow said, waving Ada closer.

Ada looked at Clod nervously and she swallowed hard.

"It's okay," Clod said. "I trust shaman."

"I promise you no harm, Ada," Millow said, her broad smile wrinkling her cheeks. "A shaman's magic touches all the elements. We are gifted with a closeness to the land and sea, to fire and air. I want to know if you are made of clay, or from clay, as Clod says. I will sense this."

"All right," Ada said, taking a careful sip of tea before setting down her cup as if it were the most precious thing she'd been given. She approached and cautiously took both of Shaman Millow's outstretched hands.

Millow lowered her head, closed her eyes, and hummed. It wasn't pretty, sounding more like the drunken singing of beggars on the street. She mouthed something that didn't sound like actual words; and the hairs on his neck stood. Ada tilted her head to one side as the odd tune crescendoed into a screeching note before dropping so low it was hard to hear. The shaman's song tapered off to nothing, and Millow gasped.

"You're quite a lovely girl, Ada," Millow said appreciatively.

"Thank you, shaman," she replied with a little curtsy. "May I go have more tea?"

"Yes," she said with a chuckle.

"Is Ada… Is she…?" his mother said, struggling with words, her eyes wide with concern.

"Ada is much more than clay," Millow said. "She eats cake, drinks tea, breaths, gets scared, and has a heartbeat. I confirmed this every way I know how. She's very much alive, and very different than I was told."

"Oh?" Clod asked, surprised that someone had been talking about his friend.

"Yugen is convinced she's merely a homunculus. They are servants made of clay and not as defined. Typically, homunculi are mindless creatures, and can be especially dangerous when they're larger," Millow said, speaking slowly as if choosing her words carefully. "He also said that she was tiny. Has she…grown?"

Ada had grown, in a way. She easily stood more than four feet tall now. Her frame was a little thin, but Clod refused to make her heavy, like him. Her brown hair now framed her face in an easy-to-adventure bob that curled by her round cheeks. She hated her round cheeks, but he thought they were cute. Much of Ada was still gray, but over the ten years since he'd first made her, it had softened and paled in color. In recent months, he'd stopped worrying so much about her height and focused on those colors enough that splotches of blue had appeared around her dress. It took a lot of effort, but he was getting closer. Even though it wasn't very becoming, she was thrilled at his progress.

"Yes, I'm able to use more clay now," Clod said. "I think my sculpting needs to be better, though."

"I see," Millow said. "So, will you be a sculptor, like your father?"

"No," Eidy said.

"Yes," he said at the same time before shooting his mother a look.

"His father had a passion for sculpting," Eidy explained, trying to stare him down. "He died young, of the wasting sickness. But, I think it was his passion, how much of himself he poured into his work, that actually killed him. Clod is a baker. He makes amazing cakes for Mr. Haim."

"I've heard," Millow said before slurping more tea. "How old are you?"

"I'm thirty-seven," Eidy said with a frown. "More or less."

Millow laughed at this, slapping her knee, and rocking back and forth several times. "I would think less. Thirty-seven is not young, and you seem filled with life, child."

It was odd hearing his mum referred to as a child, but Shaman Millow could have been fifty or five hundred, it was impossible to tell.

"Shaman, I like the tea," Clod said, almost politely. "But, why are you here?"

"Clod," Eidy said in her most motherly tone.

Millow held up a hand, and Eidy took a step back. Millow leaned toward him and looked into his eyes. "I need your help, Clod," she said. "I had hoped to help you in exchange, but I only have a little something to trade."

"I don't understand," Clod said.

"The council believed that I could possibly teach you something that would help you do the magic that you do," she said. "If Ada were clay, or a homunculus, I may have been able to offer you more. But as I thought, your magic is not my

85

magic, and there is only a little I can do to help you progress. That said, I still need your help."

"No," Eidy said, dropping to her knees before Shaman Millow. She grabbed the woman's hand with both of hers. His mother's face was stretched with panic. "The war. Please don't make him go to the war."

Millow's face became still, and her eyes cold as a frozen lake. She raised her head slightly, looking down at Eidy as if she were a beggar.

"War?" Clod asked.

"I realize you're out of school, but I'm surprised you aren't aware," Millow said, pulling her hand free from Eidy's grasp. "Do you know of the different factions?"

"A little," he said.

"Necromancers, Demonologists, Neuromancers, and others have conspired to overtake our lands," Millow said, her voice stiff. "An evil has been growing in our world. We don't know where they come from, and we aren't winning."

Clod glanced at his mum, who seemed torn between anger and fear. Her fists clenched tightly, but her eyes were filled with worry.

"How can we help?" he asked.

"Oh, child," she said with a smile. "Thank you for your bravery, no matter how blind it may be. How old are you, Clod?"

"Nineteen," he said.

"How have you kept your son from being drafted into the war?" Millow asked his mum.

"Yugen wrote a letter to the local regiment, telling the captain that Clod harbors dark magic," she said. "I didn't argue because Clod's not a fighter."

"Yes, he is," Millow said. "And so are you. We fight for what we want, with what we have. It's called survival, and nothing to be ashamed of."

"He's my…" Eidy sobbed.

"I know what he is," Millow interrupted. "And I would not send someone so…unique into war."

Eidy nodded but said nothing.

"Please stop making my mum cry," he said firmly. Clod stood and balled up his fists. Ada stood beside him and did the same. "What do you want from us?"

"Noret was a spy. He retrieved information from the enemy that could help end this war," Shaman Millow said. "He was brutally tortured, and escaped, but died from the wounds. I need you to bring him back to life long enough for him to tell me what he knows."

His stomach wrenched, and Clod felt slightly nauseous. Ada had just woken up, and should've been here for days. He didn't know if he could bring the spy to life, but even trying would make Ada go away until he woke her again. It wasn't merely a matter of being selfish; he needed his friend now more than ever. People in town had grown increasingly hostile to him since he'd gotten kicked out of school. Haim had helped him weather it, the old malgam having experienced something similar when he moved to Durgoon. At least now Clod understood it was because they thought he was from an evil faction—but that was like knowing someone kicked you in the shin for the wrong reason—it still hurt.

Ada took his hand and looked him in the eye. "It's okay. I'll be back in a few weeks...if you don't mess it up."

"Hey," he said, unable to hold back a smile. He loved it when she teased.

"I don't understand," Millow said.

"It's like the puppy," Ada explained. "Clod brought her back for a short time, but I went away. He may not be able to help your spy, but even trying will probably do the same."

"Oh," Millow said, looking at each of them.

"Clod," Eidy said, wiping her hands on her skirt. "If Shaman Millow came all the way here for your help, it's important enough to make the sacrifice. But it's your decision."

It wasn't his decision. He saw that look in his mother's eyes, in Shaman Millow's eyes, and even in Ada's eyes.

"Where?" he asked, trying to keep the defeat from his voice.

"There's a cart just outside," Millow said.

"Ada," Clod said. "You should probably stay here."

Ada shook her head and kept her death grip on his fingers. He couldn't have been more grateful.

"Let's go," Clod said.

Clod took shuffling steps—so Ada could keep

up, of course. He certainly wasn't walking slowly because he feared seeing a dead body. He was a man now, and shouldn't fear death. Especially someone else's death. But really, up to this point, the only thing violent he'd ever experienced was being pushed over or falling on someone. He'd seen the results of several bar fights that had rolled out into the street, but they hadn't deserved anything more than a wince. This was death caused by violent acts. Sweat beaded on his forehead, and his mouth became so very dry.

Clod took one step out of the cottage before shock knocked him back a step into his mum. He'd expected to find a simple cart and a body lying in it. Instead, a dozen armed knights stood at attention around a covered wagon that boasted armored war horses. A magician leaning against the wagon abruptly stood, nudging an illusionist wearing a pink frock. Another old shaman nodded respectfully while a druid peered at him warily. This wasn't an entourage; it was a war party.

"What have you brought to my home?" Eidy asked.

"It was necessary," Millow said, her face stern and her presence commanding. "The result of this mission could save thousands of lives."

"Do we need to make more tea?" Ada asked.

Millow stopped and abruptly turned to face the clay girl. "I adore you so very much," she said softly. Millow looked up at Clod. "Keep doing what you're doing. Please."

He could only nod. Nobody ever visited the cabin, and this was a little overwhelming.

"I couldn't hear them," Eidy said. "Throughout your entire visit, I thought we were alone."

"I muted any sound outside the cabin," Millow said. "It's something I do with air. I didn't want to alarm you."

"Oh," Eidy said, placing a hand to her mouth.

"Please, Clod, come with me," Millow said, her low voice gentle. He took her offered hand, and she led him to the back of the wagon.

A thin red sheet of handweave lay over a body that seemed very small and still in the back of that large, covered wagon. He glanced at Ada, who seemed transfixed, staring at the form. Millow drew the sheet away, revealing the face of a middle-aged man. Wisps of dark hair barely covered his balding head. His scarred face was sunken from death, which seemed to leave him in a restless sleep.

"How long has he been dead?" Eidy asked.

"Several days," Shaman Millow said. "We tried masking the scent with flowers, but it really only helps if you don't breathe."

"I'm not sure…" Clod said, his heart racing from the mounting expectation. His stomach clenched as the stench of death and decay reached his nose, forcing him to turn his head away.

"You can do this," Ada said. "I know you can, but it will take everything."

Clod's heart became so heavy it must have landed in his stomach, and he could only bring himself to nod.

"I'm sorry," the shaman said, placing a hand on Ada's shoulder.

"It's okay," Ada said. "This is important."

"Ada, it was a pleasure to meet you," Millow said. "I hope to see you again one day."

"I would like that very much," Ada said sincerely. "Please bring more tea."

"You enjoyed that," Millow said, "did you?"

Ada nodded vigorously.

Clod held Ada in a sincere hug. They clapped hands once, twice, three times and then kissed cheeks. He blushed, and smiled before facing the wagon.

"What was that?" Millow asked.

"A friend thing," his mum said fondly.

"Oh," Millow said, sounding bemused.

Clod studied the man's face, and the body. It was much larger than Ada, and he wasn't sure he could do what she wanted.

"What do you think?" Shaman Millow asked.

"I don't think I can bring him back," Clod said. "Not all of him."

Millow thought on this for a moment. "What about some of him?"

"Wut?" Clod asked in surprise.

"I need his lungs and his mouth," Millow said. "I don't need his legs."

"It's not right," Clod said hesitantly.

"Please," Millow said.

Clod took a final look at Ada, who smiled at him fondly, nodded once, and closed her eyes.

"I'll try." He tore his gaze away and stared at the dead man lying in the cart. Placing both hands on the man's face, he infused life into the body. Nothing happened.

"I don't think I can," Clod said, pulling his hands away.

"Clod," Ada said. "Stop it."

"But…"

"You have to do this," she said firmly. "It's okay. I'll be back soon."

"I hate this."

"Me too," she said. "But you promised me you would always try. That you'll give more than you take."

Clod set his hands on the face once more. The man's skin was cold and oily. Clod tried not to think about it, tried to breathe without smelling, squinting in concentration. He willed, and he willed, and he willed. To his dismay, Ada went still, but that meant he was close. His breathing shallowed, and his heart beat so hard it felt like his chest would burst open. Clod let out a grunt.

"No!" the dead man shouted.

Clod jerked back, and Millow rushed forward, gently pushing him aside.

"Noret, it's Millow," the shaman said.

"Where am I?" Noret asked in a panic. "I was…oh gods, I was being tortured by demons, and now I'm here. I can't move my legs!"

"You're safe now," Millow said softly, patting his cheek. "You're safe. Tell me what you learned."

Noret looked stark. Paler, if that were possible. His eyes darted around maniacally while his head thrashed to and fro. After a very long minute, Noret took a deep breath and squeezed his eyes shut, his face became somber. "Am I…am I dead?"

"Yes," Millow said.

"Gods damnit," he said loudly, rolling his head back. "I thought I was invincible."

"So did I," Millow said. "So did the council."

"So, I'm really not alive?" he asked.

"You're alive enough," Millow said. "You can still be a hero."

"There's no profit in being a hero, especially now," he scoffed. "How long do I have before the clouds of Alberon?"

Millow glanced at Clod, who shrugged.

"Fine," Noret said, sounding defeated. "I'll tell you what I learned, Millow, and then I need you to settle some debts."

Millow leaned in as Noret whispered in her ear. Ada was already a pile of ash, and a hot fire of anger flared in Clod's chest. He despised that he had to give her up to help save people who feared and hated him, even if it was the right thing to do.

"So, we need to go to Oyeret?" Millow asked.

"That's where they'll meet to make final plans," Noret said.

"Thank you, my Noret," she said. "Did you learn how they turned so many to the dark?"

"Somehow, children of the dark infected

adults," he said. "I don't know who was tainted by evil, but it's everywhere. Darkness has spread to all of the towns."

Millow thought on this before finally saying, "I will settle your debts."

"How much longer must I lie here?" Noret asked sternly before a wry smile covered his gaunt face. "There are adventures to be had in Alberon, and this delays my fun."

Clod had never taken life. It was always given as a gift, and usually to Ada. But this wasn't a life; it was barely a half-life. Millow nodded at him, and he immediately drew in. Noret gasped, and returned to being still. The life energy returned to Clod's body, but it made him feel sickly.

Millow stared at the ground for long moments. "You, and Ada, may have saved us all," she said, her voice more gruff than normal. "Thank you."

"Sure," Clod said with a heavy sigh, not quite feeling it. This had been the right thing to do, but his heart wrenched with pain every time Ada went away. "Shaman?"

"Yes, Clod," she said.

"Can you help me?" he asked. "I want Ada to stay longer…forever."

Millow looked at him and nodded in understanding. She knelt and grasped a handful of the ash left behind by Ada. Closing her eyes, Millow muttered some of those words he didn't understand. Thankfully, they weren't accompanied by another song. Long moments passed, and everyone remained silent as she did whatever it was shamans did. Clod sucked in his lips, holding his breath in anticipation.

"She's not even here," Millow said in disbelief. "I sense no life. This isn't even clay. It's merely ash."

"Yeah," Clod said, the knowledge weighing down his large shoulders.

"I can help, but not the way you want," she said.

"Oh?" he asked. Hope teased his despair like a pinprick of sunlight peeking out through a storm.

"Your magic is as special as your friendship with Ada," Millow said, her features softening. "It's a beautiful thing, and I will let the council know this."

"Okay," Clod said, wondering how this helped. "But how do I make my magic work better?"

"This is hard to explain, but it comes from you, Clod," Millow said. "When I call on the elements, it takes every bit of concentration, and will, and confidence I can muster. I also have to believe in myself. All schools of magic are this way. As you continue to grow in understanding of your power, and your need becomes stronger, she will stay awake longer. I believe that there will come a point when she won't go away."

"Really?" he asked.

"Yes," Millow said, placing a hand on his arm. "But I'm sure you can understand, that isn't something I can teach you."

"I understand," he said, not completely disappointed.

Shaman Millow snapped her fingers and reached out. The other shaman scrambled forward with a large book and placed it in her hand.

"You are a life-giver, and an artist, and those are beautiful things. They are beauty that comes from inside you, and you have to believe in this," Millow said with a sigh. "While I can't tell you how to do your magic, I would like to give you this gift."

He wanted to sigh, and roll his eyes. How could a book possibly help him with anything? It was dusky brown, thick, and well-worn. Reading wasn't his specialty, but with concentration, he could make out words if he had to.

"Techniques of Master Sculptors," he read aloud. Frowning, Clod opened the book and flipped pages. The tome was filled with hundreds of drawings that detailed body parts. It showed what tools to use, and how best to sculpt with them. His heart warmed with hope that this could help him make Ada look more like he envisioned her.

His mum coughed loudly enough to catch his attention.

"Oh, uh, thank you," Clod said.

"You're most welcome," Millow said. "I will also be leaving you with some tools similar to those found in the book."

"Really?" he asked, excitement completely washing away any disappointment.

"They are the finest in the land," Millow said with a nod as she took a heavy pouch from a knight and handed it to Clod. He fumbled with the book until it closed, and she rested it on top. "As you become more adept at sculpting, you will also find more work. Your help here will not go unrecognized, and if you ever decide to stop making cakes, cities across the land will commission you for sculptures. I will see that it happens."

"Thank you, shaman," he said.

"And one last thing," she said, removing a leather pouch from her belt and handing it over. "Tea for Ada."

"Oh," he said, swallowing hard. It was the nicest thing anyone had done for his friend. "She'll love this."

"Let's see this poor man to rest," Millow shouted to the troops. The magician, druid, shaman, and accompanying guard scrambled onto horses and fell into formation.

"Shaman," Clod said. "Will we see you again?"

Millow gave him a long, genuine hug, wrapping her arms around as much of him as she could. She pulled back and smiled in a grandmotherly way. "I would like that very much," she said. "This war is far from over, but in time, I promise to try to visit again."

"Thank you, Shaman Millow," Eidy said.

Millow nodded, approached a stout pinto, and mounted with a grunt. Without another word, the troops left their tiny home and slowly made their way down the wooded path. Clod and his mum watched in silence, standing close to each other. It was a surreal moment to have their hidden, lonely cottage visited by such an entourage. One he would never forget.

Silence covered their home like a blanket, only interrupted by the familiar sound of trees creaking in the wind.

"Quite an adventure," his mum said. "You did a good thing, Clod."

"Thanks," he said, glancing from the book to the satchel of tools he held.

"And now?" she asked.

"I'm going to start gathering clay," he said with a big grin.

Age 22

"You know Mayor Yugen's rule," his mum warned as Ada opened the door. "Stay out of town. We aren't allowed anymore."

"How could he possibly have been elected mayor?" Clod asked, incredulous.

"People make rash decisions in war time," Eidy said with a hint of worry. "Maybe he's not the man we want, but hopefully the one we need. We'll find out."

"Find out he's going to destroy us all." Clod harrumphed.

"Clod," Ada shouted in glee. "It's winter again!"

"Wut?" he asked, stepping out of their house and taking in a deep breath of frosty air.

Ada held out a hand and watched as heavy, white flakes piled up.

Clod tore his eyes from the odd sight and looked up at the sky in disbelief. "Mum?" he called out.

Eidy stepped out and immediately hugged herself for warmth. She frowned as she looked up, only to get an eyeful of flakes. "What did you two do now?"

"I opened the door," Ada said, racing forward and skidding across the slick surface of the path. "It was just summer…or was it? How long have I been asleep? Did you forget me?"

"No, I…" He held up a hand, but was too slow to block the tiny ball of snow that struck his forehead.

Her laughter was childlike and innocent, which was misleading since she was already preparing another snowball. Ada was five and a half feet of quick sass and wiry limbs. She looked more human than ever, and he gazed at her with pride. Her straight brown hair, which now reached her shoulders, was pulled back in an action-ready ponytail. Her large brown eyes glinted with mischief, always. Her skin was now a paler shade of gray—and in a shadowy room, she looked like a teenager who spent too much time inside. If anyone looked too closely, though, she wouldn't pass. Her eyelashes stuck together, and her ears were boxy and a little uneven. She was missing fingerprints, and arm hair, and toenails—he had a list. But the longer she lasted, the more progress they made, and she was lasting longer. They now enjoyed three days adventuring and two nights sculpting the next Ada before she went away.

"Quit staring like you're buying a pig at market," she warned, packing the snowball with both hands. "You're almost out of time to defend yourself."

"Maybe I *should* make you a pig next time," he said, smushing up the end of his nose with his finger and snorting loudly.

"It's on," she said, clumsily hurling the weapon while digging at the thin layer of snow for her next.

"Kids," Eidy said in her dangerous mum voice as the snowball whizzed by her cheek.

"I'm not a kid," Clod said. "I'm twenty-two."

"Then act like it," his mum said sharply.

"Yeah, Clod," Ada said in a singsong voice, brushing off her hands and placing them on her hips.

He stuck out his tongue just as a strong gust of warm wind slapped a leaf on it. Ada was laughing again as he brushed it off and spat the taste away. A cold wind bristled his hairs before it went hot as their wood stove. The snow at their feet melted in the sudden warmth, making Ada kick at damp leaves in disappointment.

"It's like the weather can't decide," he said.

"This isn't good. It's supposed to be summer and only summer," Eidy said. "We should go to town."

"All of us?" Ada asked hopefully.

"Yes, let's get our coats on, Clod," Eidy said curtly. "We're leaving now."

By the time they'd donned their winter garb

and reached the end of the long path to town, winter had won the battle, and thick flakes of snow covered their clothes. Yesterday had been so hot the only thing he'd wanted to do was sit in a shady pond. This was an unnatural cold his body wasn't prepared for, and it seemed to get painfully worse as they progressed.

"I don't think I like sn-snow anymore," Ada said, rubbing her hands together. "It's c-cold."

"That's good," Clod said. "You're able to feel more."

"That's not good," Eidy said. "She doesn't have warm clothes. She never needed them."

"You can have my coat," he offered.

"Thanks, Clod," Ada said through chattering teeth. "I'll be fine, and I don't think we can roll up the sleeves enough to make it fit."

"Right," he said, doing his best to shield her with his large arm. "Where do we go, Mum?"

A sudden gust of wind pelted them with hard flecks of snow. Both Ada and Eidy closed in, burying their faces against his sides.

"The town hall," Eidy said, her lips turning blue.

"Stay close," he said. "I'll get us there."

The storm went from bitter to vicious. The wind picked up, slicing with a blade of sleet that made it almost impossible to see. The casual five-minute walk to the town hall was becoming a twenty-minute trial of life and death. Halfway to the hall, Ada collapsed. Clod picked her up, opened his jacket, and did his best to draw her close.

"I hear something," she shouted, her teeth chattering.

He stopped to listen. Between the cries of wind and the crashing of sleet against his numb ears, he could barely make out the pathetic, high-pitched mewling of an animal.

"We don't have time," Eidy called.

"Clod," Ada pleaded, pointing at a shifting pile of snow.

Ignoring his mum, he reached into the drift and grabbed a furry bundle of kitten. It was tiny in his hand, scratching and biting in fear—but he didn't let go. As gently as he could, Clod shoved the cat into a large pocket. To his surprise, it didn't leap out—and he desperately hoped it wouldn't die in his coat.

"We need to go," Eidy shouted, tugging at his arm.

"Haim," he replied, nodding to the bakery back down the street. "We need to go back for him."

His mum looked defeated, but nodded in agreement. They slowly trudged through the snow, which was now so thick it felt like hours had passed when they reached the shop. The display window was destroyed, and snow gathered inside as if the floor were covered in white frosting. It was still cold inside, but at least it was a respite from the driving winds.

"Haim," he shouted.

"Here," Haim said from behind the counter,

his low voice shaky.

The baker huddled behind the display, shivering beneath layers of blanket. Ice coated his forehead and tusks, and his green skin was a mottled brown. The old malgam didn't look good.

"Where's Melda?" Clod asked.

"Wife's safe in the cellar," Haim said. "There isn't room for both of us."

It was everything Clod could do not to snort out a chuckle. There was plenty of space in the cellar for both of them, if he took the time to remove the stores. Clod had stocked and restocked that room more times than he could count. It was just like the old malgam to put his shop before his life. But really, what did Clod know? The shop was Haim's life.

"Come with us to the town hall," Clod said. Sweat dripped down his cheeks. He had acclimated enough to the blizzard that this room felt almost warm in comparison.

"I can't leave my shop," Haim said, slurping around his teeth.

"Yuh," Clod said, nodding and looking around at the mess. "Someone might steal some cake."

Their eyes met, and both men burst out laughing. Not only in remembrance of Clod and Ada's transgressions, but there was nobody in the world who would fight through this blizzard for a frozen pastry. Not even Clod.

"I'll slow you down," Haim said. "Malgams don't do well in the cold."

"You won't last if you stay," Clod said sincerely. "I'll carry you if I have to."

Haim peered at him dangerously. Clod stared coolly, with one hand offered until the baker took it and stood.

"Eat cake," Haim said. "It's already destroyed and will keep you warm."

Without hesitation, Clod dug his fingers into a snow-covered beauty and clawed out a giant handful. He gorged himself as quickly as he could, shoving it into his mouth like a wild animal. Haim was right, he did feel better—and in his heart, he'd always known cake would save his life.

"By the gods," Eidy said, "this is so good."

"Your son did this every day before Yugen became mayor," Haim said with a tight smile. "You should be proud."

"Always," Eidy said with a nod.

"Eat it," Clod said, handing a piece to Ada. "You love cake."

"I don't feel very good," she said in a small voice. "I'm sleepy."

"Please," he pleaded.

She took the piece and nibbled on it while he watched, and worried. She was supposed to last for days, and something about the storm sapping her life like this felt wrong. Ada was very much a part of him, not only because they were such close friends, but because he willed life into her. If she went away because of this unnatural storm, he didn't think he could bring her back.

"Don't sleep, Ada," he said. "No matter what."

"Okay, Clod," she said. "I'll try."

"You'll do," he said firmly.

She looked at him in surprise, eventually nodding and taking another bite.

He dropped a piece of the cake into his cat pocket before turning to the others. "Haim, behind me. I'll carry Ada, you hold on, and keep my mum close."

"Go!" the malgam said, gripping his shoulder hard enough to make him wince. Those enormous arms weren't for show.

The cold that numbed his muscles would've frozen them solid if not for their battle against the thickly packed snow. Sleet stung his ears while the wind deafened him. His mum collapsed, and he stopped long enough for Haim to lift her shakily.

"Go, boy," Haim shouted. "We do this!"

Time passed slowly in a blinding blur of white where minutes felt like days. Clod's brain must've been partly frozen when they finally reached the town hall, because he couldn't remember how to open the large double doors. Haim nudged him aside to work the latch, and together they dragged a door open against a hill of waist-deep snow. A furnace blast of warmth poured from inside that was every bit as shocking as the sudden wrongness of winter. It took all his strength, every remaining bit, to fight the door closed—and then he was shocked again by the silence.

He didn't remember setting Ada on the floor,

or collapsing beside her in exhaustion until the gruff cat tongue licking his face brought him around. It took long moments for his senses to return, and then he wished they hadn't. The room was stifling, and every bit of his exposed skin seared with windburn. The first thing he heard sounded like the annoying buzz of a thousand bees but at a much higher pitch. The second thing made his heart skip a beat.

"Help," a small voice wheezed from the Great Chamber. "Help me."

He would've known that voice anywhere. Ried. The worst of the bullies who'd picked on him throughout school.

"Please," Ried whimpered. "Oh gods."

"This just keeps getting better," Clod said, his voice dripping with reluctance as he shakily pushed himself up.

They should hurry, but despite the pleas from his former classmate, it took a while to gather themselves. They'd come to the town hall for sanctuary and understanding. Instead, it was almost too calm, like they'd found the eye of the storm. No wonder they were the only ones here.

The heavy burden of decision weighed on Clod as all eyes fell on him. "It sounds like Ried, from school. We should go see," Clod said. "Maybe he just twisted an ankle. That can really hurt."

They just nodded at him, listening to Ried cry out in that weak voice. It made the back of Clod's neck tingle with fear. It was hard to fathom that something awful could be happening to one of the most powerful, capable jerks he'd ever known.

The bully had been the very opposite of Clod. Almost as large, but in a muscular way that made his admirers swoon. He'd been born with the chiseled jawline of a hero, and the fair complexion of a saint. His eyes were crystal blue and sharp as his wit. Ried also held the great power of a storm mage, a weathermancer like no one had seen in a century. He was, of course, Yugen's favorite, possibly of all time. In private, Ried would occasionally be friendly to Clod. In public, the bully led the charge when it came to pecking orders, always finding new ways to ensure Clod fell in line, all the way to the back.

Clod had often wondered why someone like Ried would extend one hand in peace while striking so hard with the other. Maybe it was because he'd injured Ried once, but surviving Clod's clumsiness had only seemed to bolster the bully's rank. His nemesis had great power, adoring fans, good looks, intelligence, and it still wasn't enough to stop him from picking on Clod. His mum had tried explaining that Ried was the most insecure person she'd ever met.

"Don't assume someone else isn't struggling," she'd said. "You'll never know their demons."

It took Clod a long time to understand how this was possible. Ried had everything. He could've led armies, but instead he sought to please the masses. Eventually, Clod had pitied his almost-friend who'd never found happiness in what he was gifted.

"Why are we the only ones here?" Ada asked.

"Maybe there are more people in the Chamber," Haim said, slurping awkwardly around ice melting from his tusks.

"That's right," his mum said nervously. "They're probably in there with the elders."

It made sense, and everyone nodded while looking at Clod, their eyes filled with the same doubt that troubled his heart.

"Let's go see," Clod said, trying to sound more confident than he felt.

Ada and the cat led the way down a wide hallway. They took slow, cautious steps toward an ornately carved, wooden door—stopping every time Ried cried out. When they finally arrived, Clod was wary to enter. Ada wasn't.

The clay girl opened it, gasped, and immediately stepped away.

"Oh no," Eidy exclaimed.

Haim cursed under his breath, and placed a hand on Clod's shoulder.

It had been five years since his last visit to the Great Chamber. The room had made Clod feel small during his first visit, and now he felt tiny. The circular, domed room that was three times the size of his home should've been filled with people seeking shelter. The eight elders should've been sitting behind the high bench, preparing to save the day. That would've been comforting. That would've given him hope.

His hope sank into a pit of fear as he stared at

Ried, the only person in the room who seemed alive. The bully hovered five feet over the floor, in the center of everything. His legs and arms were spread wide as if tethered by invisible ropes. Beams of white light shot from his hands, meeting at a point directly over his head before blasting straight upward. The raw brightness was hard to look at, like lightning that didn't go away, leaving white echoes in Clod's vision. The spell vibrated with power, whining painfully in his ears as it shot through a new hole in the domed ceiling.

"Ried?" Clod called out.

His old classmate wore steel armor that practically glowed blue-white. It hung loosely on his wasting figure. He appeared to be withering away like a dried leaf in late fall. Ried's face was gaunt and wrinkled as though from age or sickness. Even more frightening than the spell, or his wasting condition, was Ried's eyes. They were wide with fear from whatever was happening, and empty at the same time, as if it was all too much for his mind to grasp.

"He's making the storm?" Haim asked.

"Ried's a weathermancer," Clod explained. "He's a jerk, but I never thought he was evil."

"Did he kill the council?" Eidy asked, her voice shaking as she pointed.

Below Ried, four bodies in dark brown robes lay around a red, square symbol marked on the white floor. It was six feet across and glowed dully. The square contained what appeared to be letters scribbled on top of letters—none of which he recognized. They formed something that smelled delicious and made his eyes stare longingly. He just wanted whatever it was the red offered. Didn't he deserve it after their long trek here? The fact that he didn't have it already made his muscles quiver, and a slick sheen of sweat covered his face.

He took a step forward when a sharp slap across his mouth forced his gaze away from the symbol. Vertigo made Clod stumble back into Haim's strong arms, and breakfast churned uncomfortably in his belly.

"Clod," Ada shouted.

"Yuh," he said, shaking his head. "Did you hit me?"

"Yuh," she said mockingly. "Don't look at the thing on the floor."

"Right," he said, slowly pulling away from Haim and steadying himself. "That's some dark magic. It must be making Ried cast the spell."

"How do we stop him?" Haim asked. "Pull him down?"

Clod gently pulled his arms away from the constant tugging on both of his sleeves. His mum and Ada finally stopped, and he looked at his mum.

"Clod," Eidy said, her voice heavy. "You know what you have to do."

"Get him," Ada said with a nod, well-versed in Clod's grievances with Ried over the years.

"Do…what?" the old malgam asked.

"I give life, like I do with Ada," Clod said. He closed his eyes and reluctantly admitted, "I can also take it."

"Oh," Haim said softly.

"I don't want to," Clod said. "He bullied me all through school, but that's not enough to kill someone. But, if he's the one doing this..."

Haim said nothing, looking at him thoughtfully with cloudy green eyes. Clod shivered with reluctance, and taking a deep breath, slowly stepped forward.

"You don't always know what makes people do things," Haim said, speaking each word carefully around his thick tusks. "You never know their demons."

Clod turned around. Both he and his mum faced the large malgam.

Haim looked as serious as death. "Do the right thing, Clod. You always do," he said, patting him on the arm. "Almost always." He winked.

Nothing obstructed his path, but it felt like an eternity passed before he reached Ried. He kept his eyes on the floating man, refusing to look down. His heart raced as every step took more effort and his feet became colder. Was it Ried? Was it the evil symbol? Or was it Clod? He grunted at his own weakness and tried shaking it off before facing his classmate. The armored man hanging in the air was just within arm's reach.

"Help me," Ried said weakly. "Clod, I'm sorry for everything. Please help me."

"Only one way I know how," Clod said, reaching toward him.

A small part of Clod, the smallest, wanted to jerk Ried from the air and clobber him. The urge was strong enough to make him hesitate. Even though revenge was tempting, he really didn't want to kill Ried. There had to be another way. Killing him might be easiest, but it didn't feel right. The bully was a floating corpse who struggled to talk, to move. Despite his condition, his haunting eyes flitted to a crumpled pile of brown cloak lying on a corner of the red square symbol.

"What are you waiting for, Clod?" Ada called. "Do it."

Clod ignored her and shuffled over to the body, covering his view of the glowing red mark beneath him with a hand. He rolled the robed mass over with a foot. The figure sprawled, and the robe fell away, revealing the face of Yugen.

Mayor Yugen was breathing but unconscious, and Clod now considered ending both of them. Who would know? His mother, Ada, and Haim would understand more than anyone. If killing Ried and "accidentally" killing Yugen saved the city, all would be forgiven, and he would be the hero. It was more than a little tempting.

He glanced at the other cloaked figures, each lying on a different corner of the square. Yugen was the only one who appeared to be breathing. Had Ried killed them? That didn't make sense. There were no signs of lightning burns or freezing or other weather-like attacks. Ried wasn't a nice person, but he'd never been a source of evil.

He couldn't be. Ried had always wanted to be popular, and being evil wasn't very popular.

"Yugen brought me here, said it would stop the war," Ried wheezed. "All five of them did this to me…it was a trap."

Power continued flowing through the young man hovering over everything. It smelled like burned sausage, and made the hairs on Clod's arms rise. Ried wasn't the bad guy. Not this time. This spell was something else. Someone else. There were only four bodies in front of the council's bench, all crumpled heaps.

"Where's the fifth?" Clod asked.

"Look at the stairs," Ada called out. "To the right."

The tiny kitten, all arched backed and hackles, crept up the stairs like a fierce hunter. Clod followed, grateful to leave the coldness of the red symbol behind.

"Don't leave me," Ried whispered. "End this."

"Shut up," Clod said. With a deep breath, he climbed the short flight of stairs and turned the corner.

Standing behind the high bench made Clod feel like a sneak-thief. This was a place for council members, not for Clods. The elders should've been here, and he wished they were.

Behind the center seat, where Priest Muane should've been, was a small, crouched body. Hetomancer Styff wore nothing but shadows that hovered around her like a dark cloud. Her hands were raised high and pointed at poor Ried like a

114

weapon. Her arms vibrated with an unnatural power that made them hard to see. She muttered words that drew Clod in, tempting him, angering him, like the symbol on the floor.

He tried to ignore her incantation, instead listening to the awful, high-pitched buzzing from the light pouring out of Ried's hands. Clod took a small step toward Styff, and then another. Instead of his normal long gait, he inched forward, as though weighed down by stronger gravity and the power of death.

Every movement was harder than the last. He wanted to stop, he longed to collapse into a heap like the robed bodies scattered around the symbol. When Styff was only two arms' lengths away, he fell to a knee.

"You can't stop me," Styff whispered, her head down and her eyes squeezed shut. "You will fall like the others. You are nothing but clay."

The effort was draining, leaving Clod shaky, even more tired than after a long weekend of chasing Ada through the forest. Sleepiness overtook him, and his vision became clouded. He tried crawling forward, but even the thought exhausted him.

A small, cool hand rested on his. Ada.

"Never apart," she said.

"Together to the end," he said with a nod.

The kitten rubbed its tiny head against their hands, apparently not affected the same way they were. It was enough to make them both smile, and in a way, helped.

They crawled together. The inches took minutes that seemed more like hours, like weeks, each movement forward more draining than the last. Styff didn't stop her spell, and it felt as if she was drawing power and life from him now. When they finally reached her, he didn't know if he could do what he needed to.

"Do it, Clod," Ada shouted.

"Together," he said.

"How?" she asked.

"That place you go when we're apart," Clod said, his voice like gravel. "Make it like that."

Together, Ada and Clod reached forward and touched Styff's hand. When they'd been outside, in the storm, cold had enveloped his body. This was a coldness that came from inside as he drew in life from the hetomancer. He'd only done something like this once before, when he'd let Noret go. The spy had already been dead so it was easy. This was like fishing a shark from an ice-covered ocean, and the two friends howled at the effort.

Styff screamed and screamed, pressing her palms against her temples as she reared back on her knees. She glared at them, her scream silenced, then finally collapsed with a hiss.

The panic slowly leaving Clod's heart was replaced with worry that this had been too much for Ada. They'd both been crawling, and were now lying on their stomachs. His friend gasped for breath and leaned into him. She was still here, she was breathing, and he tried his best not to crush

116

her in his awkward side-hug. He sniffed deeply, and convinced himself that tears weren't streaming down his cheeks. That had to be moisture from the weather, right?

There was a crash of metal followed by a cool breeze from the open roof. Ried must've fallen, which meant he was free from the spell.

Clod ached more than after his first day working for Haim. He rolled to his back, and Ada found a place in the crook of his shoulder. The kitten crawled to his chest, turned around several times proudly as if basking in its own heroics, then plopped down for a well-deserved nap. They both chuckled while staring up at the broken ceiling. The summer sun was already breaking through the clouds while flakes of snow still fell. A gust of cool, fresh air blew away the smell of burning. The light shining down on them through the open roof was almost too much. He blinked away the snow tickling his eyelids.

"So," Ada said, wiggling deeper into his arm. "What are we going to do tomorrow?"

"I hear cat training is even harder than this," he said. "If you're up for the challenge?"

"I dunno," she said. "It doesn't sound safe."

They laughed until an enormous, shadowy figure hovered over them.

"Can you stand?" Haim asked, staring down with concern.

Clod looked at Ada. Her eyes smiled through exhaustion, and they both nodded at the malgam. Haim lifted the spent kitten by the scruff and placed it in a pocket before reaching for them with unnaturally long arms. Taking Haim's hands, they stood shakily and followed the baker around to Ried, or what was left of him.

The bully's breaths were so shallow it was painful to hear. He waved Clod in closer. Eidy, Haim, and Ada stomped out as much of the symbol on the floor as they could. It probably wasn't necessary, since the square no longer glowed, but it gave Clod and Ried time, and there wasn't much left. Clod knelt weakly, practically falling on Ried, catching himself at the last second.

"I would've deserved that," Ried said.

"Yuh," Clod agreed. "But not all this."

"I thought I was being a hero. I guess that was your job," Ried said softly. "How did it end this way?"

"You wanted to be a hero because you thought it would make people like you," Clod said. "I only did it because I had to."

"I'm sorry, Clod," Ried said.

"You're forgiven," Clod said.

Ried's eyelids fell and didn't open again. Clod held his classmate's hand and wept. They'd never been close, the man had almost always been a bully, but they also had a lot of history—and death isn't something that should be taken lightly.

"Is it over?" Mayor Yugen grumbled from the other side of the room.

"It's going to be," Clod said, standing with newfound energy.

"What…what's going on?" Yugen said, pushing himself up to sit. "What happened?"

"You did!" Clod squeezed his fists until his knuckles popped. He took lumbering steps forward as Yugen scrambled away. "Ried told us. You lured him here and helped cast the spell that killed him and brought a winter storm. Who knows how many people you killed? Now it's your turn."

Clod pulled back his fist, and for the first time ever, no one tried to stop him. Who would've? Ried may not have been the source of all evil, but Yugen was. Clod had never been so furious. Not only did he want to kill Yugen with his touch, he wanted that touch to be with his knuckles.

"It was Styff," Yugen squealed, holding out both hands. "She stole our minds and forced us to cast this spell. You know what hetomancy can do. I taught you, I taught you." His hands covered his face, and he turned away with his eyes squeezed shut.

Standing over the frightened man gave Clod a certain power. Not only was he larger and stronger than Yugen, his magic could kill instantly. There was nothing Yugen could do, absolutely nothing, and it made Clod feel…it really made him feel…like Ried.

Yugen's story was viable enough that there was a shadow of doubt. Clod knew this, just as he knew this was his one opportunity to destroy the man. He wouldn't, because it was wrong, and in a way, this was just bullying. With every remaining ounce of reserve, Clod let go of his anger and loosened his fist.

"I don't believe one word," Clod said. "But I won't kill you, because I'm better than you are."

Yugen stood, brushing off his robes in disgust.

"I'll be by tomorrow to help with the shop," Clod said to Haim. "If you like."

"I like," Haim said. "But what about the law? What about him?"

"We'll tell people what happened," Clod said. "They can decide."

"No one will believe you freaks," Yugen snapped. He then whispered so only Clod could hear. "I will have my revenge, and it will cost you everything."

Clod drew his fist once more, making Yugen step away.

"You're better than that," he sneered. "Remember, Clod?"

"I'm not," Ada said, leaning into her swing. Her fist landed square on Yugen's nose.

Yugen collapsed to his back, blood pouring from both nostrils as he blinked at the ceiling in shock. They all stared at the young woman in surprise. She winked at Clod.

"Let's go home," Ada said. "We have a kitten to train."

Age 24

"Achoo," Ada sneezed, wiping her nose with the back of her wrist. She followed up with a loud snuffle. "Ugh."

"Uh-oh," Clod said, his head whipping about. He wiped clay-coated hands on his apron, cleaning as much of the slick mud off as he could. "Are you okay?"

"I don' feel so good," she said, the words muffled by congestion.

"That...that's just," Clod said, unable to hold back a smile, "that's wonderful."

"I feel awful," Ada bemoaned. "How is dat wuderful?" She sniffed deeply.

"It means you're more human than ever," he said, approaching Ada hesitantly.

"I'b not sure I wad do be human if it means feeling like dis," she said.

Clod placed the back of his hand on her cheek. Well, more like two fingers—his hand was enor-

121

mous next to her head. "You're warm. I'd say you're definitely sick."

"Dank you, doctor," she said, rolling her eyes. Ada pulled a shaggy, hole-ridden blanket from the chair and proceeded to cocoon herself in it.

"What's this?" Clod asked, kneeling beside the chair.

"I'b still working on id," Ada said. "Id's not as good as yours, but I'b learning."

The clay form was no more than a foot tall. It was definitely a person, but Clod winced at the proportions. The sculpture looked familiar, with its large, slumped shoulders, heavy cheeks, and protruding forehead. It looked overlarge, fat even, and still blocky in the way Ada had been when he'd first made her. He wanted to find something nice to say about it, but was repulsed by the thing's shape. How could something Ada make bother him so much? He knelt closer and felt a surge of anger.

"Is that..." he said, "Is that supposed to be me?"

"Sord of," she said in a tiny voice. "You're always saying how ugly you are. I wanted to show you that you're beaudiful."

"No," he said, raising a fist to crush the abomination. "The only thing beautiful about me is you."

She moved surprisingly fast for a sick woman made of clay. Before he could smash it, she was hovering over her creation and glaring at him defiantly.

"Move," he roared, his fist shaking. "I never want to see that again. It's awful."

"Id is not! Id's the face I see every dime you wake be, Clod," she said, her pale cheeks reddening. "Id's by favorite face. I love your face."

She began sobbing, which brought on a fit of coughing. When his mum walked into the cabin, Ada was leaning over mini-Clod, coughing violently between sobs. Clod was still standing over her, shaking with anger and his fist raised high.

"What is going on?" Eidy shouted, each word sharp as a knife only a mother can wield.

"Mum," Clod said, pulling back his arm and reeling in his senses. "I...uh...Mum, Ada is sick."

"I can see that," she said, kneeling by the girl. "So, what were you going to do, hit it out of her?"

"Noooo," he said, his heart drowning in shame. "Look at what she made." He pointed at the statue accusingly.

"I see, it's a little Clod," she said. "It's lovely, Ada. You sculpt like I do."

"You sculpt?" Clod asked, dumbfounded.

"I used to," she said. "By the elders, Clod, why would you destroy her creation?"

"It's ugly," he said. "Like me."

"The only thing ugly in this home was that fist, and I don't ever want to see it again," she said, glaring at him. "Do you understand?"

"Yes, Mum," he said. "I'm sorry, Ada."

She merely nodded, and he picked her up gently, setting her down in the chair and wrapping her in the shoddy blanket.

"I really am sorry," he said, kneeling beside the chair. "It was very thoughtful."

"How are *you* feeling, Clod?" his mother asked.

"I'm fine," he said, wiping sweat from his forehead. "Ada is the one who's sick."

Ada brushed away tears with the blanket and looked at Clod with worried eyes. "Why are you sweating?"

"It's warm in here. I've been working on that sculpture for Radenbrook," he said. They both looked at him like he was covered in boils. He was used to those types of glances from people in town, but not from his mum or Ada. "What? I'm fine. Just a little tired."

"I think it's more than that," she said. "Please wash up and go lie down, Clod."

"But I'm fine, we should be taking care of Ada," he said, wondering if maybe his mum was sick too. "Why are you telling me to go rest?"

"Ada is a part of you," Eidy said. "You know this. If she becomes sick, it's a reflection of something affecting you."

"Oh," he said. "But I've got to finish the sculpture."

"There's plenty of time," Ada said with a sniff. "I'm feeling better than you look, really."

"I'm going to get the healer from town," Eidy said.

"He won't come," Clod said, his chest feeling raspy. "People still fear Yugen, even after he was banished."

"I'll persuade him," Eidy said, patting Clod on the arm. "I want you and Ada to rest."

"No," Ada said, twice as defiant as her height. "I know where to find healers. I'll go."

"But you've never met him. He's a—"

Clod dropped to a knee, suddenly overwhelmed with exhaustion. This was dumb. Why did he feel so tired? Had he been pushing that hard?

"Clod, you'll rest better in bed," his mother said, trying to help him up. "Ada, would you give me a hand?"

There was a coughing sneeze as the door closed. Ada had left without another word.

"Ada, wait," Eidy called out.

"Mum," Clod said. "What's happening?"

The room spun in a frenetic assault of heat and sweat. The floor was hard when he landed with a boom that shook the rafters, but despite the initial smack of pain, it was cool to his cheek. His vision and thoughts faded in and out like a sun behind drifting clouds. His mum had tried rolling him to his back, which made him giggle uncontrollably. When he rolled himself over, she was momentarily trapped under one of his arms, which, oddly, seemed far too heavy for him to lift. The room went dark, and he woke for a moment, calling out for Ada. Why wasn't she there? Was she gone already? He succumbed to darkness and woke suddenly to a noisy door hinge and sharp light.

A blubberous old man with reddish skin and a

bald head framed with gray hair stood in the doorway. His eyes were wild, and he mumbled something around Ada's hand, which was shoved wrist deep into his mouth. She rode on his back, her other hand clutching a long, pointy ear that was never meant to be a handle.

"I swear, healer, if you don't go in and help Clod, I'll turn your tongue...no, your entire jaw to stone," she shouted. "Now go!"

He nodded, sweat dripping freely from his cheeks, and snorted through his pig-like snout. Had she really ridden him like a horse, with her hand in his mouth, all the way to the cabin? Clod laughed maniacally as she drew it free and wiped her arm on Healer Swayloo's shoulder.

"Get off," Swayloo squealed in a wince-worthy voice. "I'll look at the boy."

Ada hopped off Swayloo's shoulders like she was dismounting a prize pony. The healer's mortally offended glare was soon washed away with concern as he knelt beside Clod.

"How long has he been this way?" Swayloo asked.

"Hours," Eidy said.

The healer reached into a pouch and drew out several spotty leaves. He rubbed them between his hands while muttering something unnatural that Clod's ears didn't really want to hear. He shied away as best he could, but Swayloo jerked Clod's head back and shoved the leaves into his mouth. Clod had never tasted a color, but somehow knew it was green. It was worse than green;

it was disgusting. His body convulsed, wanting desperately to expunge the green that soaked in like a new, warm sickness.

"What are you doing?" Ada shouted.

"Quiet, beast," Swayloo said sharply. "This one is almost dead, and I'm doing what I can to save him."

Dead? He couldn't die. Ada needed him in order to live. She would only be awake for another day. His mother was on the verge of quitting her job now that he had regular sculpting work. He had to live, damnit. They *needed* him to live!

"That's it, boy," Swayloo said with a grunt and a snort. "Push through."

Clod had once run too far, chasing Ada through the woods. Collapsing onto a prickerbush in exhaustion, unable to breathe, Clod had thought he'd died. That was easy in comparison. This was a thousand prickerbushes, probably every prickerbush on Yulth. And then it was gone, like a noisy crowd of people suddenly silenced. There was a cool blackness until his mum slowly appeared, shouting with Ada for him to wake up. Eventually, he did push through death's cobweb and woke to madness. His mother was bawling. Ada was slapping him and shouting. The red pigman doctor snorted out his spells, spittle landing on Clod's face.

"Stop," he said, pushing up on his elbows. "Stop, please. I'm fine."

They all stilled, staring at him in disbelief. The quiet in the room was only broken by the rustle of

Ada's clothes as she hugged him, and the soft, tearful kisses on his cheek. Long moments passed as he breathed sweet air that tasted so much better than green. Healer Swayloo rested on his haunches, wiping globs of oily sweat from his red face. His mother held herself, seemingly unable to speak.

"Wut happened?" Clod asked. "Wut was that?"

"The wasting," Swayloo said softly. "I'm surprised you still live."

"The wasting?" Clod asked in surprise. "That's how my dad died."

His mother nodded in confirmation, her eyes flitting up to make the briefest contact before returning to the floor.

"There's nothing more I can do," the healer said. "It's only a matter of time now."

"No," Eidy demanded, turning on Swayloo. "You can't be done."

"There is no cure for the wasting, and I've already done too much," the pigman said. He stood, holding out a shiny black hoof defensively. "Yugen, his allies, will see me dead if I do more. He hates you, all of you. Yugen says the ugliness of your evil taints our town, that you were to blame for the summer blizzard. I can't be kicked out of town like he was. I have a family."

"Fine," Eidy said, the word dripping with frost. "But I promise, Clod will live longer than you."

"I just," Swayloo said, "I just don't understand."

"What's that?" Clod asked.

"What are you?" he said, looking at all of them.

"What are any of us?" his mother asked after a long silence. "People. Beings. Creatures. Entities. All of us alive. Thinking and living. We look different, we act different, but all of us want the same thing. To live a life not threatened by others. Is it so hard for you to fathom? You, who are so different than them?"

Swayloo said nothing, staring at the floor. After a long moment, he shook his head. "I need to go."

"I agree," Eidy said sternly. She walked to the door and opened it. "Ugliness comes from hatred, and there is nothing ugly in this home."

The red pigman stood on shiny black hooves that clicked noisily with every step. When he reached the door, he turned to face them. After a brief moment, he nodded respectfully, snorted out his pig nose, and trotted away.

"How about pot pie for dinner?" Eidy asked enthusiastically.

"Really?" Clod asked, practically drooling at the thought. Gravy, meat, and pie—it was truly the best of all worlds, and by far his favorite meal. The very thought made him feel better already.

"I'll even make you three this time," she said. "But only if you both promise to help."

"But he's still sick," Ada said, clinging to his

arm.

"I'll make him better," Eidy said. "And it starts with pie."

He was disoriented and weak, as if he had slept for days and wasn't ready to wake up. It was all a bit surreal. Despite his mum's worry lines, she acted as if the ordeal had never happened. Ada didn't look ready to celebrate his recovery quite yet, a frown on her face as she stared at Eidy.

"Ada, you tell Clod about how your hand ended up in pigman Swayloo's mouth," she said, making Ada blush and Clod chuckle. "I'll run to town and get ingredients."

"Mum?" Clod asked.

"Yes, Clod," she said.

"Thank you," he said. "And thank you, Ada."

Ada sneezed, but nodded vigorously. His mum frowned at his clay friend before rushing out the door.

"She's not telling us everything," Ada said. "I'm worried you're still sick."

"Yuh," he nodded. "But mum doesn't lie to us."

"True," she said, lost in thought. She shook her head. "What was that creature?"

"He's the healer," Clod said.

"I know he's the healer," Ada said. "I got him."

"Oh, yuh," Clod said.

"I want to know *what* he was?" she asked. "Maybe you're still sick in the head."

Clod stuck out his tongue before answering. "He's just a pigman. I guess they're the best race of healers."

"You've never talked about him, or them," she said with a frown. "Are there others?"

"Sure," he said with a shrug. "Andoo, one of the boys who picked on me in school. He was a pigman."

"You never mentioned that," she said.

"Doesn't make a difference what he looks like. He was still mean," Clod said, staring at his feet. "Pigmen…they don't like being called that. The Pilaly can be pretty aggressive. The ones I've met like to argue."

"I noticed," she said dryly. "That's why I made him stop arguing."

Clod laughed and patted her gently on the shoulder. She told the story of her tongue-grabbing persuasion in extensive detail. Some of the terrible rumors of their "dark magic" had actually helped, and Swayloo had apparently believed all of her threats. Clod was both impressed and grateful for her bravery.

"Are there others who don't look like us?" she asked.

"You mean other races?" he replied. "Sure, more than I can count. Elves, and dwarves, and nessmu, and frouli, and plainta, and…"

"Wait," she said, holding up a hand. "Do all of those races hate me for being different, like Swayloo?"

"I dunno," Clod said. "Probably not all. I

guess most wouldn't even care about you. It's not about races, but the nations they come from don't like others for dumb reasons. It's complicated. I didn't pay attention to that much in school."

"So, why keep me hidden if people don't care?" she asked.

"Yugen," his mum said from the doorway with an armful of groceries. "He could never sense Clod's magic, so he assumes it comes from evil."

She set the bag of food on the table before approaching Clod and placing the back of her hand on his forehead. The worry lines by her eyes didn't go away.

"Why?" Ada asked, sniffing noisily.

"He's a smart man, but very arrogant. I don't think he understands how you two work," Eidy said, waving a hand back and forth between them.

Clod looked at Ada, who shrugged and smiled.

"Yugen came to the conclusion that if something doesn't fit into his way of thinking, it must be evil," Eidy continued with a sour face. "So, he made us out to be bad. In turn, it made him look good, which helped him to become mayor."

"Ugh," Ada said, her face contorted in disgust.

"He's gone now. The council banished him, and took his magic," his mother said. "He had a lot of friends, and they all blame us, so it's important to be careful. I understand why Swayloo was in a hurry to leave, even if it makes him a coward."

"Banished Yugen," Clod said with a smile. "Better than Learned Yugen."

"Ha!" Ada said, her laugh turning into a cough.

"Ada, are you okay?" Eidy asked. "You look tired, dear."

"Yeah," she said weakly. "I think it's time."

"Aww," Clod said. "It's too soon."

"I guess that's what happens when we both…get…sick," she said.

There was a crunching sound as the clay woman stilled. At first, she looked like an old statue with fine cracks. A cobweb crept across her like a shattered window. Clod approached, wishing he could hug her one more time as tiny bits of clay fell to the floor. He reached out and took her hand, which still seemed so small in his own. It became ash as her body fell into a pile. It hurt every time.

"You've done wonderfully, Clod," she said, gripping his arm. "Ada is quite a friend, and she's lasting longer every time."

"Yuh," he said. "I wish she wouldn't go."

"One day, very soon, she will stay and won't go," his mother said. "But none of us last forever. Be grateful for the time you have together."

"Sure, mum," he said, watching the last of the ash collapse into a pile. "I'll try."

"You'll do," she said.

His mum went about preparing the pies, humming a tune to herself while Clod dozed. He was tired from being sick, the room was warm and smelled like meat and pastry, and sleep sounded like a good idea. But every time he'd start to drift, she would wake him with an Ada question, or share a nostalgic story about his dad. Somehow, despite his exhaustion, he was able to focus when she set three pies beside him.

She watched him fondly as he gorged himself on dinner. It would've been rude to healer Swayloo to say that Clod pigged out on the feast, but accurate. He was still tired, but the ache from overeating would keep him awake for hours.

"Ada would probably last longer if you used stone instead of clay."

"Wut?" he said in surprise. "I... How does that work?"

"Clay and stone are both earth," she said. "If you carved Ada from stone, and woke her up, she would still be like us. She would be alive, with a heartbeat, and warmth, and flesh—she would just last longer."

"But how do I carve stone?" he asked, dumbfounded.

"Wait here," she said, walking to the bedroom.

She came back and handed him a large, leather roll tied off with twine. It was hard to loosen the knots with his thick fingers, and his mum's excitement was distracting. Finally, he unrolled the bundle to find worn steel carving tools unlike any he'd seen.

"They were your father's," she said, with a small catch in her breath. "He wanted you to have them when you were ready."

"But...stone?" Clod said in disbelief, looking at the tools as if they'd been touched by the gods.

"Your father's best sculptures were made from stone. Many of them can be seen around town. Some are even at the castle," she said. "Stone lasts much longer than clay."

"Sure," he said.

"Those tools weren't just your father's. They've been handed down for generations," Eidy said. "Many in our family have been sculptors. You saw their work when you were young, playing tag with Ada."

"The graveyard," he whispered.

"Yes," his mother said softly. "Let's go look, and I'll tell you about your father."

Clod really didn't want to leave their home, especially to go to that forbidden place. He still felt sick, and the only things keeping him awake were the excitement of his father's tools and a stomachache from too much supper. There was no arguing with his mum, though, so he slowly stood and followed her outside. A sense of foreboding tickled his skin until he had goosebumps, and he wished Ada were here to hold his hand. She wasn't, and he held hands with his mum instead as she led him down a wooded path.

"I would like you to listen as I tell you this story," she said. "Please don't interrupt or I'll become distracted."

He nodded obediently.

"Your father's name was also Clod," she said. "I may've misspelled it, but it was Clod. He was a big man, and like you, had a gift for sculpting. I can sculpt too, but I've never had his talent. I'm sorry for that."

"Why are you sorry?" he asked, before remembering he wasn't supposed to interrupt.

"Only because of how unhappy you've been with the results," she said. "I've never been disappointed at all."

The explanation didn't help, but he kept himself from asking more. It was obvious from her tense voice that she was upset. His mum was quiet for a while as they stepped over a rotting log and made their way down an embankment.

"Your dad worked very hard. Our home is small, but we have quite a bit of land. Everything on this side of town is ours. You've walked the breadth of it with Ada. Our land stretches between the city and the sea. And, we own the only lot of clay," she said proudly. "He fought for that, and won."

Clod bit his tongue, trying not to express his shock. It was such a great expanse, so much that he'd thought it belonged to the kingdom. They'd always lived in poverty. Why hadn't they sold just a little bit to be comfortable?

"It's not about money, Clod. It's not about things," she said, as if reading his mind. "You've never gone hungry, or without a roof. We have what we need. We also have clay for molding, and stone for carving, and they are the key."

She seemed nervous and worried, which made his heart race. Holding his tongue made his anxiety worse.

"Your father's life was every bit the challenge

yours and mine have been," she said. "Our lives have been filled with hard work that often feels thankless. You feel that way, don't you?"

Clod was hesitant to speak, not wanting to interrupt, but she'd stopped and was looking at him. "All the time."

"How do you feel when you're with Ada?" she asked.

"Wonderful," he said, warmth in his heart. "She makes it better."

"Is she worth it?" Eidy asked.

"All of it," he said.

"I feel the same way about you," she said, squeezing his hand hard. "It's not always about comfort or things. It's really about friends and family."

He nodded because it made sense. Ada was the only friend he had, and he only had brief moments to spend with her. At first, days instead of weeks, now weeks instead of months, and all of them precious. He tried hard to make the most of his time with her, because they didn't have much. If they had, maybe he would've taken it for granted. He didn't.

They reached the graveyard of statues, and she rushed him through a maze of stone figures. They moved so quickly, he didn't have time to make out faces. The statues were a mess of men and women of different sizes, all standing in peculiar poses. Clod had been to the city graveyard, but had never seen monuments like these. When they finally stopped, he stared at the ground, fearful to look up.

"Clod," she said softly. "This is your father."

She placed a finger under Clod's chin and gently pressed upward. It was like looking at a mirror of himself, but one made of white stone. His dad was every bit as huge and awkward as he was. He had the same dull expression, heavy jowls, hunched over shoulders, and hanging gut. Still, the sculpture smiled with a sort of relaxed satisfaction.

"Dad?" he asked, his throat tight.

"He was a good man," she said. "As was his father."

He followed his mother's eyes to another sculpture. It was also Clod. Not really, but so very close. Maybe thinner, with a longer nose, and curly hair. He looked down the row of sculptures and saw dozens, maybe hundreds of Clods. Between each of them were hundreds of Adas and Eidys.

Clod felt bombarded with confusion, fright, and exhaustion. These statues made no sense, how could it be possible that so many of them looked familiar. It felt like he was walking on his own grave, and he shivered at the prospect that this was where it would end. Why had his mother brought him here? He was just so tired, so very tired that he worried the wasting would take him away from Ada and his mum when they needed him so bad. She gripped Clod's chin again and pulled his face to meet her gaze.

"I love you, Clod, as you love Ada," she said.

"I had the wasting sickness, and your dad saved me. I was angry with him, at first, but in time I came to know this was the way of things. You'll become angry with me, but in time you'll understand that this is the only way I know to save my Clod. You have many years to come with Ada, and that is my gift to you."

"I don't understand," he said. The churning in his stomach wasn't from pie. He wanted to ask more, but her stern gaze told him this was a time to listen.

"Take your time with your next sculpture of her, even if it takes months. Make her every bit as real as you can." She took a deep breath, her eyes glassy with tears. "Then, the hardest part. Believe in yourself, in your own beauty. It comes from inside you, Clod. When you do believe, pour all your love and magic into Ada, and she will always be with you. Promise me."

"I promise, Mum," he said, unable to keep the shudder from his voice.

"I love you, my Clod," she said, holding onto his hand so hard it almost hurt. She reached up to his father's outstretched hand and gripped it hard. "I'm so glad I made you."

"I love you too, Mum," he said.

Life. Her life flowed into him like a cool brook on a warm summer day. It felt familiar, like when she'd tend to his scratches, or listen to him talk about his clay stories as a youth. It was so much of her love that he squeezed his eyes shut. A dizziness overtook him, making him stagger, but her grip was firm. And then too firm. And then he opened his eyes.

His mum was stone, as solid and still as any statue in the graveyard. One hand held onto his father's, their fingers intertwined. Her other hand held onto his own. And then he understood. And then, he wept like he'd never done before.

Age 27

"You are making my retirement party not fun," Haim said, his tall ear lifted mockingly. "You can't always be sad, young Clod."

"Sorry," Clod said, patting Haim's leathery green arm.

"You thinking of your mother?" Haim asked.

"Not this time," Clod said sullenly. "Ada should be here."

"She's probably upset you won't take my shop," Haim said, only half joking.

The other half of Haim's joke was filled with bitterness and a hint of resentment. Clod could bake, but he wasn't a baker. Haim had wanted, more than anything, for Clod to take over his legacy. The malgam deserved this. He'd taken Clod under his wing, as an employee, and as a son. But the shop was a gift Clod couldn't accept. Not because he didn't appreciate the significance, but because he'd finally realized what he was.

141

CLOD MAKES A FRIEND

* * * *

Clod had spent almost two years alone, without his mum, and without Ada. The first few months after his mum turned to stone was a desperate time filled with futile attempts at reviving her.

It felt like a cruel trick. He could bring back puppies or half dead bodies all day long. They were made from flesh and bone when they lived and retained some of those qualities when they died. Clod, Ada, and his mum weren't human, in the traditional sense. When he made Ada out of clay, he was unable to bring her back after she turned to ash. His dad must've carved his mum from stone. When she went away, she returned to stone, and there was nothing he could do. His magic had limitations that mocked him, making life seem that much more unfair. All of which just made him hurt worse.

When the mourning and grief finally lessened, he committed to taking some of her advice. His mum had pressed him to make Ada one final time. To carve his friend from stone so she would last.

He spent more than a year failing. The entire time was filled with struggle and heartache. He missed his mum, who would never come back, and he missed Ada, who unknowingly waited for him. He refused to bring Ada back as clay; he wanted her to stay which meant she had to be carved from stone. Figuring out how to chisel and shape with his father's tools wasn't a learning curve—it was a learning mountain, and the cost was great. Clod didn't take good care of himself as he was practically obsessed. He even sold off parcels of land to have blocks of stone delivered.

It took months more to realize why it wasn't working. One late night, after too many failures, he was about to give up. Clod just didn't understand why he couldn't carve her image like he saw in his mind. It should have been easier, because he loved Ada so much, just like his mum had loved him. She had poured all of her love into sculpting him. And that was when it came together.

Both his mum and Ada, and even Shaman Millow, had tried to convince him that beauty came from inside, but it was hard to accept when he couldn't stand looking in a mirror. He'd believed that everything about him was ugly, which made it almost impossible to make someone as beautiful as the Ada he saw in his mind. But, how could he truly be ugly if he was made from his mum's love? This realization was the lifelong hurdle that kept him from succeeding, and understanding meant he could finally do it. Clod chiseled the barest of grooves into Ada's toenails. He carved out hairs on her legs and arms. Each finger bore unique fingerprints. One eye was a little higher than the other, and one ear slightly lower. She had moles, and dimples, and imperfections, and blemishes, and everything that made one human. After hundreds of failures and angry frustrations, he finally, finally made her as Ada as he could. Then he willed, and willed, and willed until his heart hurt and he gasped for breath. And then she woke. And then she was Ada. His Ada who would always stay and never leave.

* * * *

"I hope you know I tease," Haim said, his tone becoming a little sly. "Mostly."

"I wish I could take the shop, but Ada and I have more sculpting business than we know what to do with," Clod said. "She wants to take on apprentices to help. It's overwhelming. I don't even know where the business comes from."

"Rumor is that Shaman Millow tells townships to commission work from you," he said. "And after what you and Ada did to Yugen, nobody argues. You were heroes!"

"We were all heroes," Clod said, unable to hold back a smile. "We couldn't have done it without you."

"Bah," Haim said with a dismissive wave that didn't hide the smile around his giant tusks.

"Not this story again," Melda said as she came up from the cellar. "Every time you call him a hero, Clod, he stops working for a week to bask in his glory."

Haim's wife was even larger and more muscular than Haim. Clod struggled to tell them apart, except that during some seasons, Melda was a darker shade of green. Every spring, her tusks would grow from her top jaw, and then she would lose them at the end of summer. He'd been there when they came out once, and almost threw up. Apparently, tusk removal was a private matter among malgam, and she took his reaction poorly. It took weeks for the bruise on his forehead to heal. Those tusks were solid.

"Speaking of Yugen," Haim said. "Wasn't he in town several days ago?"

"Wut?" Clod asked. "But he was exiled."

"Mostly. They never proved the storm was all him," Melda said. "And there are still humans here who like him."

"You look worried, Clod," Haim said.

"Ada was going to meet me here hours ago," Clod said. "Wut if he took her?"

"He has no magic. The council leached it," Haim said with a shudder. "And she could stop him with a touch."

"Yuh," Clod said. "If she could touch him."

"So…what to do?" Melda asked.

"He was in town for a reason," Clod said. "Where do Yugen's friends hang out?"

"I'll show you," Haim said. "This bad party anyway."

What could Yugen be planning if he didn't have magic? His old teacher hated them, blamed them for everything bad that happened. How far would hatred drive Yugen? Was he planning to kill her? Had he already? With every fiber of his being, Clod believed Ada was still alive. She had to be. Clod's heart wanted to climb out of his throat as they rushed across town.

He winced when they arrived. The Hid Inn was a seedy dive of dark corners and greasy milieu. It was one of those places his mum had told him to stay away from, and crossing the threshold fueled his anxiety.

"Get out," growled a gray dwarf who was as wide as he was tall. "Your type aren't allowed…"

Haim squeezed through the door behind Clod, and glared down at the short man. He placed his giant hand on the dwarf's head and pressed hard enough to make the man yelp. His hand remained steady, the malgam's sharp nails hovering just above the dwarf's eyes, and he leaned slightly as if he'd found a new favorite cane.

"That's them," Haim said with a nod. "At the thwart game table. I watch your back."

"Who'll watch my front?" Clod said with a gulp.

"You a man," Haim said. "Be brave, and do what you have to. It's for Ada."

Clod approached the rectangular, wooden table at the far side of the room. Three people stood on both sides along the length, each of them smacking levers or shoving poles. A muscular man with oily black hair and pale skin stood at the head, gripping two edges of the thwart table as if holding onto a wheelbarrow. He jerked suddenly, rocking it from side to side as the others cheered and jeered. Despite the raucous growls, it looked like everyone was having fun.

Clod's curiosity was stamped out like a small

fire when he saw what was going on inside the table. A sizable rat scurried through a maze filled with traps. The levers were meant to force it into action, either prodding the rat forward, or jabbing it until it turned around. The poor beast looked mad with pain that abruptly ended. A prod struck the rat's back with a loud snap, making it squeal until it stopped shuddering.

"Another loss for ya, Telk," a scraggly looking drunkard shouted.

"Trollbile," Telk cursed, picking up the dead rat and shaking it. "Fah," he shouted, tossing the carcass into a steel bucket beside the table. The bucket was half-filled with dead rodents.

"You want a go?" a sweaty redhead woman asked Clod. "Game of thwart will cost you two brets."

"No, uh," Clod said around his dry tongue. "I'm looking for my friend, Ada. Pretty, with long brown hair, twenty years old..."

"No one pretty around here," Telk said.

The woman slapped his mouth, which was followed by a round of laughter. The angry muscle man smacked two coins on the game table and pulled another rat out of a nearby crate. The box was filled with animals waiting for death, and Clod's shoulders tensed.

"Please," Clod said through gritted teeth. "I think Yugen has her..."

"Move off," Telk said, holding the frightened rat up to Clod's face. "It's probably too late for that one anyway, boy. Yugen's probably done with her already, I gotta thank him for one less freak in the world."

Clod roared in anger, grasping the rat and drawing life from it. The creature's squeals stopped as it deflated and finally went limp. Telk stepped back into his friends, who scrambled away. Clod grasped the large man's throat and drew in the tiniest bit of life. A trickle, a drip, just enough for the man to feel it. Telk went weak, unable to stand on his own.

"I heard of you," he wheezed. His legs shook, and Clod continued holding him up by his neck.

"Tell me where Ada is, or one of your friends will," Clod said, drawing in just a bit more.

"The caves," he whimpered. "At the edge of the woods."

"Why?" Clod demanded with a growl.

"He's gonna get his magic back," he said. "Says her life can do it."

Clod's heart stopped. He let go, and Telk collapsed to the floor. He glanced around the room. Not a single person breathed, their eyes filled with fear.

"If you ever do this to animals again," Clod shouted, kicking open the crate of rats, "I will come for all of you."

The rats scurried everywhere, and he stomped over them to Haim, who released his hold. The dwarf fell to his knees and crawled away. Clod rubbed his hands together as they walked out. He felt like he needed a bath.

"You shake," Haim said. "You okay?"

"I don't like killing," Clod whispered. "Not even rats."

"It was a mercy," Haim said. "Let's go get Ada."

"No," Clod said. He stopped and turned to face his friend. "You can't come with."

"You shouldn't go alone," Haim said. "Sounds like dark magic. We should be heroes together again."

Clod couldn't help but smile, a little. He placed a hand on Haim's broad shoulder. "Please get Shaman Millow. If this is dark magic, and I can't stop him, the council will need to."

The malgam took several breaths to compose himself and let go of heroics. Age and realization finally settled in. "Be safe, son," Haim said with a nod, and lumbered off to the town hall.

Running again. Why did everything about Ada require running? His mind tried talking his legs into a brisk walk, logically explaining that he didn't want to be exhausted when he found Yugen and Ada. His heart knew Ada was still alive, and pushed his legs to move faster than ever. He was a steamy, sweaty mess when he arrived at the cave, but, to his surprise, was still able to breathe.

The cave was easy to find, at the edge of his own property. It was nauseatingly close to his home. Had Yugen been living here since being exiled? Had he been spying on them? It gave Clod goosebumps that felt like they may never leave.

A dim, flickering light at the end of the cave was enough to guide Clod. He recognized Yugen's voice as it moaned words that made Clod's skin crawl and his stomach clench. It was true. This had to be dark magic.

"Clod," Ada called out, her voice muffled.

"I'm here," Clod said, entering a room that was larger than their cabin.

Yugen stood over a squirming Ada-filled bag, dragging the tip of a sick-looking dagger along the burlap. His old teacher had lost weight and grown a goatee that was long and white, ending in a point that made his face seem angular.

"Finally," Yugen said. "It took you long enough, dolt. I couldn't have placed more bread-crumbs around town. I almost fell asleep waiting."

"Waiting for what?" Clod asked.

"It's a trap," Ada cried out. "Run!"

"Let her go," Clod said.

"Oh, okay," Yugen said, kneeing the bag.

She grunted but didn't cry. Clod wanted to. She was always so much braver than him, and he latched onto her courage.

"Over there," Yugen said, gesturing with his dagger. "Now, or she's dead."

Clod glanced over at a red, square symbol on the cave floor that made him want to retch. It was similar to the one at the Town Hall during the blizzard, and it took all his will to tear his eyes away.

"Do it," Yugen shouted maddeningly, "or I'll

kill your Ada!"

"Clod," Ada called out. "He'll get his magic back, and—"

Yugen kicked the middle of the bag hard enough to cut her off. Ada began coughing. Clod took a step forward, and Yugen grasped the sack and lifted it.

"Now," Yugen snapped.

A sudden chill overwhelmed Clod, making him shudder. This wasn't the brisk cold from a winter wind; this was a painful, achy cold that comes from being sick. He looked around the cave, trying his best to avoid the symbol. Something was wrong—not only did he feel it, he could see it. Whenever the light dimmed, even a little, shadows on the cave walls squirmed like a pile of snakes. They constantly crawled over each other, as if watching and waiting for something. There was more going on than Yugen getting to cast spells again, and Clod didn't want to be the catalyst. He needed to give the council more time to get here.

"A day of days." Yugen laughed maniacally. "I get my magic back, I get my life back, and I finally purge this town of your ugliness!"

"No, Banish-ed Yugen," Clod said.

Ada laughed at the nickname.

"What's this?" Yugen asked.

"All my life, I've wanted to beat a bully," Clod said, his knuckles popping as he balled his hands into fists. It was the sound of dry leather being stretched over brittle tree branches.

"You…you can't beat me," Yugen said. "I'll kill her! I'll do it!"

"My mum always told me no. She said violence was never the answer. That my size and strength could kill someone by accident, and I would have to live with their death for the rest of my life. I always held back, until now."

Clod slowly, carefully rolled up the sleeves of his red tunic, folding end after end until his strong arms were revealed. His hands were calloused and rough from years of sculpting. Veins protruded along his muscles, well earned from collecting clay, and hauling flour, and carving stone. His naturally large forearms and biceps bulged in a way that made Yugen swallow hard.

"I'll take her life," Yugen said, his voice shaky. "Or I'll take yours. Which is it?"

Yugen was lying or he'd have killed Ada already. Clod took another step forward, glaring at the man. Despite his rising anger, his heart beat steadily as a clock. He took in deep breaths that escaped his nose, sounding like a bull readying to charge. It was as if years of chasing Ada through the woods had accidentally made him healthy.

"Do you even understand me?" Yugen shouted. "You always were a terrible student."

"You were an awful teacher. Baker Haim was *my* favorite," Clod said. He moved forward, slowly, to draw out the conversation. Every step landed with a loud thump that made the earth shake. If an ancient oak tree could've walked, if a mountain could've taken a step, they would've had the same presence as Clod lumbering to Yugen. "He taught me that there was only one way to beat a bully—by taking away whatever it is they hold over you. Maybe it's their strength, and they need to be physically beaten. Maybe it's their voice that needs to be ignored, or silenced."

Yugen shoved the tip of his dagger into the bag, making Ada cry out. Clod stopped moving, stopped breathing as her blood spilled to the ground. Shadows swarmed the blood, darting in and out, feasting on her life.

"There's no beating me, or any of us," Yugen said. "Even when you stopped Ried from destroying the town, Styff and the others didn't die. Not completely. They still thrive in the shadows. It took me a long time to realize that you and yours," he nodded at the Ada bag, "are the key to bringing them back. They're ready for their revenge after all these long years, and they thirst for your life!" Yugen shouted, spittle flecking his beard. He jabbed the dagger at the bag again, making Ada yelp. "Is it going to be you, or her?"

"Fine," Clod said. "I guess you win."

"Clod, no," Ada pleaded.

"Life is about give and take. Sometimes you give," Clod said, lowering his head. "And sometimes you take."

"Oh," Ada said, a hint of wonder in her voice.

Clod moved to the middle of the symbol, each step making his guts wrench. It was a distraction he didn't need, and he squinted, bracing for what was to come.

"Get him," Yugen cried. "Cast his soul into a pit of darkness that falls forever!"

"What's happening?" Ada called out.

"I've been gathering my fallen brothers and sisters for the last several years. They're shadows of their former selves, barely alive," he said with a sneer. "But all they need is the smallest pinprick of life to come back."

"But how can you bring them back?" she asked. "The council took away your magic."

"They should've taken my hands, too. I can't cast, but I can still draw." He laughed. "Clod has enough magic to trigger the spell. Why don't you see for yourself?" Yugen released Ada from the bag and kicked her to the floor so she was out of reach. "It seems I was mistaken after all. Clod is actually good for something."

Shadows around the room dove at Clod like a shark feeding frenzy. Every attack was a stab of despair, and depression, and hatred, and cold, each of them trying to draw life. It hurt more than anything he'd experienced. He wasn't a hero, he didn't want to face this brutal attack, and he hated every minute of it, even when he started laughing.

"Wut?" Yugen asked, his expression of maniacal glee washing away.

"I feel them, all of them," Clod said. "This isn't just your four casters. There are dozens. They're cold, and weak, but very, very alive."

Like a whirlpool, Clod drank in every living shadow that attacked him. They slowed, trying to turn away and fight the current, but Clod became the sponge that absorbed the ocean. The cloudy face of every black shadow he drew in contorted into a silent scream and disappeared.

"Stop," Yugen pleaded. He raised the dagger high and rushed toward Clod. "You're killing them."

Ada wrapped herself around Yugen's foot and rolled. There was a loud snap as his ankle bent the wrong way. He cried out in pain, collapsing to the cave floor. She lay still, grasping her ribs, and taking short breaths. Blood dribbled out from between her fingers where the dagger had struck.

"Hurry and finish, Clod," she whimpered. "I don't feel so good."

"I don't think I can stop them all," he said. "There are too many."

There weren't just dozens of shadows, there had to be hundreds. Each of them contained the tiniest morsel of life, but combined, it was enough to feed a town of Clods and Adas. A shadow bounced off him, and then another. He'd hit his limit. There were just too many to take in. When the mostly-dead realized this, they began striking at him. It was a pummeling worse than any he'd experienced in the schoolyard. Shadows leaped from the walls, diving at him, each blow harder than the last.

"Clod," Ada said weakly, reaching for him.

"Ada," he wheezed. "Watch out."

Yugen had rolled around until he could position the dagger over her neck. With both hands wrapped around the hilt, he raised it as high as he could and drove it down.

"*Stehp ern en fru,*" Monk Syt shouted from the entrance.

Yugen stopped moving, stopped breathing, the dagger mere inches from Ada. The shadows stilled, no longer attacking Clod, their faces frozen. All over, parts of his body throbbed with pain, and he gasped for breath.

"I bring the thunder," Shaman Millow cried out.

There was, indeed, thunder. An ear-shaking boom made the cave shudder and dust fall from the ceiling. Cracks appeared on the living shadows, as if she'd broken a mirror. Another rumble of thunder, and frozen shards of shadow fell to the ground, breaking on the floor like icicles landing on a sidewalk. The onslaught of sound continued until the cave floor was covered in black, and the monsters were gone.

"Nobody move," Cleric Dyes said in a high-pitched voice. "Don't touch them."

Dyes rushed forward, scooping the dark crystal remains into bags that never seemed to fill completely.

Wizard Pyle limped forward, leaning heavily on his staff. He muttered incantations with one clawed-hand directed at Yugen. "We got here in time," Pyle said, gasping for breath. "Yugen is still without magic."

"Ada," Clod said, rushing forward. "She's hurt. Please help her."

Priest Muane was already kneeling by her side,

mumbling something soft and comforting. "That should help."

"Thanks," she squeaked. Without another word, she leaped from the cave floor and into Clod's arms, where they remained in silent relief for long moments.

"You were so brave," she whispered. "I'm so proud of you."

"You make me brave, Ada," he said. "I love you so much."

"I love you, Clod," she said.

Someone placed their hand between his shoulders, their touch warming his entire chest as if he'd been lying in the sun for a long time. When he finally set Ada down, the priest removed his hand from Clod's back. His smile didn't match the worry in his eyes.

"It's good to see you again, Clod," Shaman Millow said, patting him roughly on the arm. "And you too, Ada."

"Thanks for coming," Clod said.

"Your mum tried to tell us Yugen was evil," Millow said. "I didn't believe her. I'm sorry."

"I didn't want to believe either," Clod said, staring at the frozen body of Yugen. "I knew he was a bad person, but didn't know how bad."

"What do you mean?" Pyle asked.

"When I got here, he said he was bringing back his people," Clod said. "I thought he meant the four from the town hall, but there were a lot more. It felt like hundreds."

"The banished," Muane whispered.

CLOD MAKES A FRIEND

Clod and Ada looked to Millow for answers.

"Styff's attack was going to be the first of many," she said. "We believed she'd controlled Yugen and the others. There are councils in every major city, so we spread the word. The councils all stopped the attacks in time."

"It was the end of the war," Muane said, and his dry voice held a hint of exhaustion. "Or so we thought. Most who were tainted by the dark seemed to die when their magic was removed, but the dark must've kept part of them alive."

"There were so many," Clod said.

"They'd been planning for decades," Pyle said, hands falling to his sides. "They went after the learned in every town. Our foes must've planted dark seeds in their classrooms. Many learned were tainted by the darkness they sensed, eventually infecting some of their students like a plague."

"I absorbed life from all those shadows," Clod said. "Am...am I...tainted?"

Cleric Dyes placed a hand on Clod's forehead, closed his eyes, and muttered a spell. After several moments, he asked, "How do you feel?"

"Full, Master Cleric," Clod said. "But hungry for food. I don't understand."

"You are practically brimming with life," Dyes said, eyeing him up and down. "But I sense no evil in you."

"It seems you have a choice ahead of you, Clod," Shaman Millow said.

"What's that, shaman?" Ada asked.

"Well, with all that life, you and Ada could probably live forever," Millow said. "Or…"

He understood, and nodded.

"What does she mean?" Ada asked.

"Apprentices," he said with a broad smile.

"Oh," Ada replied, her eyes wide with excitement.

"It's over now," Millow said. "We are in your debt once again. We will have to keep Yugen alive long enough to find out if there are others. He'll resist, but we have ways of finding out. You'll be glad to know, they hurt."

"Good," Ada said darkly.

"Just one more thing," Clod said, nodding to Yugen. "Can he hear me?"

"He can," Pyle said.

"Mum taught me that violence isn't the best way to beat a bully. You beat a bully by taking away their power," Clod said with restrained calm. "I took away your darkness… I beat you, Yugen, just like I said I would. And you can never hurt me again. Let's go, Ada."

She looked at Yugen's broken ankle and smiled contentedly. Taking Clod's hand, she led him out of the room.

"You okay?" he asked.

"Yes," she said. "You?"

"Yuh," he replied. "But we're late for a party."

"I love parties. Will they have cake?" she asked. "You deserve cake."

"We both do," he said with a broad smile.

Age 57

Boom!

Clod opened his eyes as quickly as he could. He felt his years, all fifty-seven of them, begging to go back to sleep. Raising his head took a lot of effort, and he corrected that mistake by letting it crash back to the pillow. His body wasn't quite ready to get up, even if his mind disagreed. So, he lay there, taking deep, raspy breaths—giving his body the time it needed while his mind did other things. It was just a boom, and he was allowed to be old.

Discomfort was a natural and unfair condition that seemed to come with age, and compared to nearly everyone Clod had met, he was old. Most of the council had passed on and been replaced, save for Priest Muane and Shaman Millow. His mum hadn't lasted this long, nor had his dad. But, still, here he was. A few bullies from school still lived, but seemed worse off than he felt. Other than them, and Ada, everyone else from his youth was gone. It was a cold reminder that his was a long life for not being a shaman or a priest.

Thud. Rumble rumble. Screams. Silence.

"Wut was that?" Clod asked. Apparently, this was not a morning for waking leisurely. "Ada, are you okay?"

He rolled out of bed, creaking as much as the wooden frame, and stood as tall as he could. His shoulders hunched a bit, like his old mentor Haim. He missed the malgam, and his wife with the painful tusks. Clod pulled at the door, which shuddered against the floor and stopped just short of letting him out. He really needed to fix this one day.

"Don't you ever, ever do that again," Ada commanded from outside their cottage.

She was using the voice that made Clod wince. Ada hadn't drawn that weapon on him often, but he'd always taken it to heart, even when it was pointed at someone else. Hopefully it was pointed at someone else.

"Ada?" Clod called, pulling at the door with all his considerable weight until it gave just enough to squeeze through.

The front door opened smoothly to a beautiful summer day, so bright he could barely see. He blinked sunshine and sleep from his eyes to take in chaos. Directly in front of his cottage, smack in the middle of the clearing, stood an eight-foot-tall, rectangular stone. It hadn't been there yesterday.

"Wut's this?" Clod asked, looking around.

A dozen or more people of various shapes, sizes, and colors stared at the monolith in awe. Their lack of response was irritating, and he was going to ask again until his eyes finally found Ada. One hand on her hip, and the other one pointing to the top of the stone. His eyes followed her finger.

"How's this, boss?" a young girl peeped.

"I told you," Clod said, shading his eyes with a hand, "don't call me boss."

Maya stood on the stone, her dark skin glistening in the sunlight. Her arms crossed, she had a proud gleam in her eye. She reminded Clod of Ada when she was twelve, and he did his best to hide his amazement with the sternest glare he could muster. She avoided his gaze and looked over the edge. The sudden realization of heights washed away her haughty demeanor.

"Uh," she said. "Can you help me down?"

He looked at Ada, who shook her head.

"Why is there a giant rock in my front yard, Maya?" Clod asked.

"You said you were gonna teach us how to carve stone soon," she said excitedly.

"Yuh," Clod replied. "In a month or two, with small rocks. Very small rocks."

"Last week you told us to think big," she said. "That we could do anything!"

"I was hoping you'd do 'anything' later," Clod said. "And not in front of my house."

"Sorry," she said, sounding distraught. "I

162

could move it back."

"No," he said, holding up his hands.

His no was echoed by the surrounding families, and Maya began to cry. He reached up, slowly, stiffly, high enough to touch the top. She sat on the ledge, inched forward, and fell into his hands. Several onlookers gasped in relief. Clod pulled her in close for a comforting hug.

"It's okay, Maya," he said, patting her wiry hair. "We'll use this when it's time."

"Really?" she asked with a sniffle.

"Yuh," he said. "It must've been very hard to move."

"It was," she said, cracking a smile. "It took me hours."

"You're the only one of us who can do this," he said. "It's a gift. You have to be careful with it so nobody gets hurt. Okay?"

"Okay, Clod," she said.

He set Maya down beside her sister Jayra, who had tears streaming down her cheeks. Jayra was several years younger, and every bit as adorable as her sister, except for the furious tear-stained glare and balled up fists.

"What's wrong?" Maya asked.

"Mr. Cupcake Frosty Alabaster Timms," she said, pointing to a spot under the rock. "He was going to be here for another day."

"We're not supposed to make animals," Maya whispered, as if they all couldn't hear her.

"But Mr. Timms is my best friend ever," Jayra said.

"There are always exceptions for best friends," Clod said, nodding at Ada.

"I'll help you work on a new Timms tomorrow," Maya said. "I promise, Jay Jay."

"Thanks, Maya," she said quietly.

"Let's go talk," their mum said sternly, leading them both by the arm. She turned her head about to mouth a 'sorry' to Clod and Ada.

"We'll postpone morning classes," Ada said to the crowd. "Let's meet after lunch."

Clod and Ada watched as families walked down separate winding paths to their own cabins nestled away in the woods. Each of them spoke with their children, some followed by dogs or cats, a few goats, and one rabbit. All frightened, or happy, or distraught. All of them living. Clod's heart swelled.

"Clod?" Ada asked. "Are you crying?"

"They're just all so beautiful," he said. "They are filled with beauty, and ugliness, and anger, and love. They can do anything, or they can do nothing, and I love that, and I love them all."

"You're a sap," Ada said, shoving her shoulder into him. "Your mum would've been proud."

"Yuh?" he asked.

"Yuh," she said mockingly. "All that life you absorbed in Yugen's cave, and you could've done anything with it, but you did this. You could've lived forever. We both could have."

"You're upset," he said.

"Forever with Clod sounds pretty wonderful," she said.

"Adaaaaa," he said, looking at the ground.

"I love you, Clod," she said.

"I love you, Ada," he said quietly.

"It was the right thing to do," she said. "We were the last, and now we aren't, and that's... What's on your face?"

Clod struggled to focus on Ada's eyes as the ground leaned to one side. With a deep breath, he gathered his few reserves until everything steadied. It wasn't a new feeling, and he'd assumed it was because of them, his people. Creating so many 'apprentices' had used up almost all the life he'd absorbed in the cave. Almost, because he'd kept a little for him and Ada. He didn't want to go away as quickly as his mum, or dad. He'd earned the right to be a little selfish. The reward was great, and he had no regrets, but now he was tired.

Clod wiped sweat from his face and looked at his hand. It was covered in ash. He sighed deeply.

"Clod?" Ada asked, her chin quivering.

"It's time," Clod said. "Ada, let's go visit my parents."

"No," she said, grabbing his hands, and squeezing her eyes shut.

The familiar coolness of life, her life, flowed into him. He immediately pulled away.

"Clod," she said, reaching for him.

He dodged her grasp, and dodged it again. It was like every game of tag they'd ever played, and he couldn't help but chuckle.

"Please, Clod. Let me share a little more," she

said. "I don't want to be here without you."

"You've been keeping me alive?" he asked.

"Well…" She looked down at the ground.

"That's why your hair is gray," he said in surprise.

"I don't want to lose you," she said softly.

"Ada," he said, touching her cheek. "I'm tired."

She looked at him with tear-filled eyes.

"It's past my time," he said. "I'm beyond exhausted. I hurt every day. We aren't meant to live this long."

"But, but you're my Clod," she said, clutching him in the fiercest of hugs.

"And you're my Ada," he said, pulling her close. "You always will be."

Long moments passed, and Clod strained to draw away. His very bones felt stiff, every breath was a chore, and he knew it was time.

"Bring me to my parents," he said. "We need to hurry."

"You hurry. I'll just walk," she said with a little sass.

"I never was able to keep up," he said. "But the chase has been wonderful."

She nodded and took his hand, tears streaming down her cheeks. Every step was harder than the last, and he worried they wouldn't make it. It hurt, all of it, but it didn't matter. Life had been worth the effort, and he'd gotten everything he'd put into it, and more. Not only had he saved his people, he had Ada.

They arrived at his parents' statues, and he noticed something. His mum was still holding hands with his dad, but his dad must've been holding hands with his own mum, and so on. Every statue in the graveyard was connected, forever. He would never be alone, and this gave him comfort.

"Clod?" she asked.

"I never noticed when we were here playing tag," he said. "But they hold hands just like we do."

She nodded, swallowing hard.

"I love you, Ada," he said. "Thank you for being my friend."

"I love you, Clod," she said.

"Come to me when it's your time," he said. His arm was stiff, and he had just enough left to reach out and hold his mum's hand. He squeezed Ada's hand with his other and smiled. "I'll be here waiting."

* * * *

A dog barked, and footsteps grew louder as several people approached.

"Found her," someone said.

Ada didn't care. More than anything she just wanted her Clod to come back. She looked up at his beautiful stone face. It was hard to see, her eyes blurry from tears. Nothing had hurt as much as this, and she finally understood why it had taken him two years to bring her back after his mum had gone. Ada held onto his hand, which was cold and smooth to her touch. She willed life into him, but nothing happened. He wasn't here any-more. It happened just as he'd said it would, which didn't make it better.

Everyone from the village had gathered near-by. Their people, his people, each of them mourning in their own way. He'd been a part of them all, and every one of them hurt like she did. Almost like she did. She stood, wiped her eyes, and gathered herself. He was right; they were beautiful, all of them. Maya pushed her way through the crowd and took her hand.

"I'm sorry, Ada," she said, her voice cracking. "I'm so sorry. Is there anything I can do?"

Despair blanketed her mind as grief wrenched her heart in pain that couldn't be healed by any-one but Clod. He had made her, they'd never been apart, and she wasn't whole without him. Part of her despised him for leaving, but more than that, she loved him. Somewhere, deep down, she knew they'd be together again. But that didn't help, not even a little. It had taken Clod two years to bring her back, but she refused to wait that long. Ada let go of Maya's hand, grasped both her shoulders, and looked her in the eyes.

"Get me some clay."

THE END

About the Author

David J. Pedersen is a native of Racine, WI who resides in his home town Kansas City, MO. He received a Bachelor of Arts degree in Philosophy from the University of Wisconsin - Madison. He has worked in sales, management, retail, video and film production, and IT. David has run 2 marathons, climbed several 14,000 foot mountains and marched in Thee University of Wisconsin Marching Band. He is a geek and a fanboy that enjoys carousing, picking on his wife and kids, playing video games, and slowly muddling through his next novel.

To learn more about David and his writing please visit his website:

www.gotangst.com